The Haunted Lighthouse

A LIN COFFIN

COZY MYSTERY

BOOK 6

J.A. WHITING

To hear about new books and book sales, please sign up for my mailing list at: www.jawhitingbooks.com

For my family, with love

CHAPTER 1

With her boyfriend, Jeff, pedaling beside her, Lin Coffin rode her bicycle along the bike paths that ran next to Milestone Road on their way to the east side of Nantucket island. White puffy clouds dotted the bright blue sky and the air was clear and warm. They had packed a lunch of chicken sandwiches, cookies, and fruit and planned to eat once they'd arrived at East End Lighthouse and had a chance to walk around the area. Jeff had been hired to work on the restoration of both the lighthouse and the keeper's house and he and Lin wanted to check things out before the whole crew arrived on-site and started the job.

Rounding a bend on the pathway, Lin and Jeff could see the red and white lighthouse standing tall on a knoll in the distance. Passing by green fields and shade trees, the two pedaled up the hill and parked their bicycles in the bike rack next to the small gravel parking lot. A pleasant breeze danced over the ocean and blew a strand of Lin's long, brown hair against her cheek. To their right was a sandy cliff with a steep, abrupt drop to the ocean and a low beamed railing kept visitors from getting too close to the treacherous drop-off.

East End Lighthouse had been built in 1820 and the brick and granite conical structure, wider at the bottom and tapering to a slightly narrower upper section, rose seventy feet into the air. Shortly after it was constructed, the lighthouse was painted white with a wide bright-red central band. Around 1940, the light's Fresnel lens was replaced with a high-power spotlight and the lighthouse became fully electrified flashing it's bright white beam every seven seconds. The light could be seen for over twenty-six nautical miles. A ten-foot tall, black cast iron light-tower stood at the top of the structure with an iron platform encircling the section just beneath. Standing on the platform provided a view that stretched for miles in all directions.

A small, one-story keeper's house built of wood and brick stood a few hundred yards from the lighthouse and an original wooden barn was located behind and to the left of the keeper's house to the south. The old barn had fallen into disrepair with one side looking lopsided and its paint so faded that most of the structure was now bare wood.

Lin stood staring up to the top of the lighthouse. "Every time I come here, I think it's so beautiful, the colors, the shape, the height." A door stood at the bottom of the structure and a small window was built into the side at the top just under the black platform. "There isn't a keeper anymore, right? Just someone who comes by and checks on the place?"

Jeff nodded. "That's right. The lighthouse is automated now, has been for years. Someone makes a bi-monthly check on the light or comes out when there's a report that the light isn't functioning properly."

Even though they'd both visited the light many times and already knew many of the historical facts, Jeff took Lin's hand and they wandered around the grounds, stopping to read the information plaques that stood here and there explaining the long history of the lighthouse.

"What will the renovation work entail?" Lin asked as they moved closer to the towering structure.

"For me, a lot of it will be interior work." Jeff pulled at the visor of his cap to better shade his eyes from the glare of the sun. "The lighthouse stairs are shaky and loose and some of the cement has fallen away from the brickwork. The watch room floor needs repair and some places on the floor of the platform need to be shored up. A good portion of my work will involve restoration of the keeper's house and the barn. The Conservation Commission plans to open the house and barn to the public with historical displays and with docents who will give talks about lighthouses in general and the specifics of this one."

"How long is everything supposed to take?"

Jeff laughed. "You know how timelines go. A big crew will work for about three months, and then, depending on how severe the coming winter is, a smaller group of us will be here for another month or two. It's an involved project."

Lin glanced around. "Well, you couldn't ask for a lovelier spot to spend your work day."

Jeff smiled broadly. "I have to admit I'm excited about this. I can't wait to get started."

Lin and Jeff returned to the parked bikes and removed a small cooler bag and a blanket which they carried to the bluff overlooking the Atlantic Ocean. After spreading the blanket over the green grass, they sat down to enjoy the lunch and the beautiful view out over the blue expanse of sea. Waves crashed against the rocks below, sea birds cried as they darted overhead, and sailboats floated over the blue surface of the ocean with their billowing sails catching the wind.

The warm gentle breeze refreshed the couple after their bike ride to the lighthouse and after finishing his sandwich, Jeff rested back on the blanket and closed his eyes for a few minutes while he and Lin talked about going to the beach early in the evening with Lin's cousin, Viv, and her boyfriend, John, and then to Viv's for a barbecue dinner.

Lin bit into a salted caramel cookie and shifted around on the blanket to watch the boats sailing by when a cool shiver ran over her skin. She rubbed her bare arms trying to warm them when she suddenly stopped what she was doing realizing that the cold sensation that was chilling her wasn't from a breeze or from an afternoon drop in temperature.

Holding her cookie near her mouth, Lin glanced over her shoulder to the lighthouse grounds looking for the source of the cold air as the sensation around her grew stronger. Her eyes moved to the lighthouse, the keeper's house, and the old barn and then her gaze swept over the grounds. The peculiar feeling of coldness contained an almost biting sensation and Lin knew that it was not coming from atmospheric changes. This kind of cold sprang from one thing only. Ghosts.

Lin's ancestors were among the early founders of the island and she'd inherited a certain skill from some of them. She was able to see ghosts and when they appeared, they usually needed something from her. Since returning to the island early in the summer to start a new life, Lin had helped to solve several mysteries and the ghosts had offered direction and assistance to her in their special way ... they never spoke to Lin, they just showed up and she would have to try to interpret their appearances.

Lin sighed and bit into her cookie as she continued to look over the lighthouse's grounds and buildings. The cold surrounding her began to dissipate and, even though she knew better, she started to relax thinking that maybe it *was* just a current of cold air passing by over the ocean. Even though she tried to push the thought of ghosts from her mind, Lin had a growing sensation of unease running through her like the buzzing of an electrical current jumping around in her body.

Jeff opened his eyes oblivious to what was going on with his girlfriend. "Want to walk around some more?"

Lin nodded and they headed down to the keeper's cottage where they walked the periphery and peeked inside through the grimy windows. The house was a two-bedroom cottage with a kitchen and a fireplaced sitting area. Because of the glare and dinginess of the glass, it was hard to see into the rooms, but as Lin and Jeff made their way around the house, they eyed a small wooden dining table and two chairs, the frame of an old bed, and a few dishes and cups sitting on a shelf over the kitchen counter. At one of the windows, the curtains hung in tatters like a cat had jumped up and clawed them to pieces.

"I thought the condition would be worse." Lin stepped back from the window. "Imagine how nice it will be when it's been refurbished. It will be great to take a tour when the work is all done."

"I bet there's plenty more history to know than we've read." Jeff leaned down and checked the stone foundation as they moved to the next window. "We should ask Anton what he knows about the lighthouse and the keepers who worked here."

"Oh, I bet Anton would love to talk about that." Lin chuckled. Anton Wilson, a retired professor, was an expert on Nantucket history having written many books on different aspects of the island's past.

When Lin moved close to the next first-floor window, a whoosh of cold air hit her in the face and she almost gasped from the suddenness of the sensation. Glancing around to see where Jeff was, she was glad he was at the back of the house and didn't see her recoiling from the icy blast. Lin didn't want to try and explain what was happening when she had no idea herself. Creeping to the dirt-streaked pane of glass, she peeked inside to see only a small wooden desk tucked next to the wall of the small room that seemed to have been the keeper's tiny office. The sunlight reflected on the glass and made it difficult to see the room clearly so Lin began to turn away just as something caught her attention. She turned back and pressed her face closer to the window. Thinking for a moment that she'd caught sight of a person dashing out of the room, she shook her head and scoffed at her imagination. *It's just the light shining in through the dirty windows causing some shadows.*

"Lin, want to go down to the barn?" Jeff pointed down the hill.

She smiled and nodded and the two headed to the old barn. They spent a few minutes walking around the large structure taking in the years of damage.

"Can it be salvaged?" Lin asked.

"Kurt says yes." Jeff smiled. "I would have thought it was too far gone, but Kurt brought in an expert and they went over it together and the barn is definitely worth restoring. The trustees managed to hire some superstar architect for the project. He knows what he's doing."

Lin tilted her head to look up at the barn's cupola. "I'm glad it's able to be restored. It would be a terrible shame to lose such a great piece of history." As soon as the words were out of her mouth, a strange feeling of unease gripped her and she reached up and ran her finger over the antique horseshoe necklace that hung from her neck.

Back at the top of the hill after their inspection of the property, Lin and Jeff packed up the lunch bag and attached it to Jeff's bike. Just as Lin was about to swing her leg over her bike, a sudden blast of cold air blew her hair into her face and she reached up and pushed it out of her eyes. Lifting her gaze to the top of the light tower, she saw the shimmering face of a middle-aged man behind the glass windows staring down at her. A scruffy gray beard covered the man's cheeks and chin and he wore a sea captain's hat on his head.

Lin, slowly, and as discreetly as possible, lifted her hand in greeting and a sense of overwhelming sadness hit her squarely in the chest. She couldn't pull her eyes away from the glimmering man in the tower.

The ghost raised his hand to her ... and then the particles of his being broke apart and began to glow as they swirled round and round with increasing speed. The atoms sparkled and sparked ... and then the man was gone.

CHAPTER 2

Lin and Viv bustled about the kitchen preparing side dishes of rice, salad, and baked broccoli with garlic and oil. The deck table was set with white and blue plates and jar candles had been placed on the railings and down the steps. John, Viv's boyfriend, was outside preparing the grill for the evening's dinner of chicken kabobs and flat bread with pesto, goat cheese, and sun-dried tomatoes.

"Have you been back to the lighthouse since you and Jeff took the bike ride out there last week?" Lin's cousin, Viv, asked as she stirred the rice in a big pot on the stove.

"I haven't." Lin arranged the broccoli in the baking dish. "The crew has only been working at the lighthouse for a couple of days so I'm eager to hear how things are going."

Nicky, Lin's little brown dog, let out a bark and then he and Viv's gray cat, Queenie, raced for the front door.

Viv watched the animals rush away. "Jeff must

be here since the welcoming committee just went to answer the door."

Lin laughed and wiped her hands on a dish towel. "No one can sneak up on those two."

Jeff called a greeting from the front of the house and, carrying a big glass bowl filled with fruit salad, he walked into the kitchen with the dog and cat proudly trotting ahead of him. Lin and Jeff shared a kiss.

When the food was ready and everyone had settled around the table, the foursome dug into the food and chattered about their work days.

"Too bad we had to skip going to the beach, but I had to meet that client. I think I might have a buyer for the house out in Madaket." John, a seasoned island Realtor, smiled widely thinking about the large commission that might be coming his way.

Viv scowled. "I hope the money isn't going to *another* boat upgrade."

John laughed. He had recently sold his old boat and bought a bigger one. "I'm happy with the boat I have, but I *am* planning on buying a new guitar." John and Viv played in a band a few nights a week and John's guitar needed to be replaced.

Lin passed the platter of broccoli to Jeff. "How are things going at the lighthouse?"

"Everything just got underway a few days ago. Some things are being removed like parts of the observation deck that runs around the section near the top of the lighthouse. It's interesting to see. I've been working in the barn." A strange look passed over Jeff's face.

"What needs to be done on the barn?" Viv asked.

"A whole lot. It's a mess. The main beam needs to be replaced, then we'll be shoring up the walls and the roof. The plans are terrific. That architect they hired is a master. The barn is going to be such a great asset to the finished project. The trustees want to use the space for lectures and classes and even hope to hold some musical performances and plays in there." Jeff looked down at his dinner plate.

Lin could sense some unease coming from Jeff and she reached over and squeezed his hand. "Is everything going okay?"

Jeff made eye contact with Lin and nodded. "Yeah."

Lin tilted her head. She could tell that Jeff wasn't sharing everything with them. "But...?"

Jeff let out a long breath. "Some weird things have been going on."

John's eyes widened and he leaned forward. "Weird things? Like what?"

"Little things. A guy put his tool box down someplace and when he went back to get it, it was in another spot. Someone removed several slats on the observation deck and then at the end of the day, the guy went back up there and most of the slats were back in place."

Viv's hand flew to her chest. "What? How can that be? What's going on there?"

Lin asked, "Is someone playing a joke on the workers?"

Jeff shrugged a shoulder.

"Do you think one of the guys could be trying to sabotage the work?" Lin's voice was tinged with concern.

"Wow, if a guy is messing around like that, it's going to add to the timeline and to the cost of the project." John narrowed his eyes. "Why would someone do that, though? What would be the motivation? If it's just a joke, it isn't very funny."

"And how is it done with the other workers around?" Viv's voice was high-pitched. "How could anyone do things like that without someone seeing?" She took a quick glance at Lin and then looked back at Jeff. "Is it dangerous for you to be working on this job?"

Jeff's eyes widened. "I think ... I think it's okay." He turned his head to Lin.

A shiver ran down her back and she swallowed hard. Lin had mentioned to Viv and Jeff that she'd seen a ghost when they'd visited the lighthouse a week ago, but she'd downplayed the whole thing in the hopes that the ghost didn't want anything from her. Viv and Jeff had known for a while that she could see spirits, but John had no idea about her skill, so she had to keep quiet about it. Lin placed her hand on Jeff's arm. "Keep your eyes open. Be careful. Just in case."

The four talked for a while longer about the odd happenings at the lighthouse project and everyone agreed that whoever was behind the sabotage would be found out pretty quickly. Conversation turned to the approaching Labor Day weekend and the island's fall festival and after enjoying the cheesecake dessert, John excused himself to return to his office to work for an hour on paperwork in case the offer on the house in Madaket came through.

When she was sure that John had left Viv's house, Lin looked from Viv to Jeff. "There's that ghost at the lighthouse."

Viv almost dropped her glass. "I knew it. I knew that ghost must be behind the antics at the lighthouse."

"I didn't say the ghost was responsible for messing with the project." Lin pushed some strands of hair from her eyes. "That stuff is probably being done by someone who is still alive."

"Why don't you think the ghost is behind it?" Jeff asked.

"I just don't get the sense that he's up to trouble."

Viv wrapped her arms around herself. "What *do*

you sense about the ghost?" she asked warily.

Lin thought back on the short interaction she'd had with the spirit. "I sensed loneliness and a terrible sadness coming from him."

Viv ran her hand over her forehead. "Then why doesn't he cross over to the other side? There'd be lots of other ghosts there to interact with if he crossed over and stopped hanging around on planet Earth."

Jeff looked at Lin. "Why would a ghost not cross over?"

Lin shrugged. "I'm not sure. It might be because the ghost died unexpectedly or the ghost might have suffered a violent death. Violent circumstances could prevent him from crossing to the other side. It could also be that there's unfinished business of some kind that must be tended to." Lifting her hands up in a helpless gesture, she added, "I don't know anything for sure. It's only what I've read or heard."

"I wonder how long that ghost has been hanging around?" Viv asked.

"And who is he?" Jeff questioned. "What did he look like?"

Lin pictured the face at the window of the lighthouse. "I could only make out his face. He was looking out of the window and he was far away from me. He had kind of an oval-shaped face, a grayish beard ... not long though, short on the face.

He was wearing a cap, kind of like a ship captain's hat." Lin thought for a moment. "He had bluish-gray eyes."

Viv gave her cousin a skeptical look. "Bluish-gray? That's very specific. He was up in the lighthouse. How could you see his eyes so clearly?"

Lin stared at Viv. She was right. *How did I see his eyes?* Lin shrugged a shoulder and shook her head a little back and forth. "I don't know, but I know for sure that his eyes are blue-gray."

"Do you know his name?" Jeff asked gently.

"No. That's all I know. I don't know who he is or how long he's been at the lighthouse or when he died."

Viv got an idea and straightened in her chair looking eagerly from Lin to Jeff. "Anton might have some books on the lighthouse keepers who lived and worked there. Maybe the books have some pictures or drawings of the keepers. You could look through them and see if you recognize the ghost."

"That's a great idea." Lin smiled. "And Anton might know some of the history of the keepers." She rolled her eyes and chuckled. "What am I saying? Of course Anton would know some history." Anton Wilson was an island historian who knew and had written extensively on many aspects of Nantucket.

"I know you don't feel that the ghost is responsible for the problems on the work site, but do you think it's possible that the ghost could be angry about the work being done at the lighthouse?" Jeff considered. "He might not want people tampering with the place. He might not want all of these workers buzzing around. Could he feel threatened by the renovation work and be causing the troubles?"

"It's possible." Lin didn't really know for sure, she only got the sense the ghost was lonely and that he carried a deep and heavy sadness in his heart. It was certainly possible that the ghost didn't want the workers there and was tampering with the tools and the repairs and renovations, but that wasn't the sense she got from him.

Lin had never encountered an angry ghost or a ghost who interfered with the living. The only spirits she'd come across were those looking for assistance from her or who offered some help to right a wrong that had occurred. She hoped this lighthouse ghost didn't want to hurt the workers who had recently arrived at East End Light to make the needed improvements to the structures.

A flutter of concern ran through Lin's body as she turned with worried eyes to Jeff and took his hand. "Please be careful at the site. We don't know why the ghost showed himself or what he wants. It could be dangerous ... even if it's *not* the ghost who is responsible for what's been happening."

Viv frowned and placed her hand against the

side of her face. "You need to be careful *especially* if it's not the ghost. At least if it's the ghost, maybe Lin can talk to him and get him to stop messing with the work. If it's a living person who is causing the trouble...." Viv let out a groan. "Who knows what he's up to."

And, Lin thought, *what is the reason?*

CHAPTER 3

Lin sat at the old wooden table in front of the fireplace in the kitchen of Anton Wilson's antique Cape-style house sipping from a glass of iced tea. Anton sat across from her with his right arm hanging down to pat Nicky's head. The dog's eyelids were closing from the pleasant scratching and he leaned his body lazily against Anton's leg.

"Very interesting." Anton adjusted the black frames of his eyeglasses. "A ghost keeper of the lighthouse." The historian pondered the news.

Lin added some details about her sighting of the ghost. "He seemed sad, lonely. That was the vibe I got from him. He showed himself just before we were about to leave. I acknowledged him with a slight wave. He raised his hand to me in greeting. His face was so serious."

"I wonder who this is." Anton went to his den and returned with several books about the East End lighthouse. "I've written about lighthouses of New England. I recall the history of the East End light, but I don't recall all of the keepers." Shuffling through one of the books, Anton peered at the some of the pages. "Here it is. A list of all the keepers who tended East End." He turned the book so Lin could see.

"There are so many names." Lin pushed her long hair back from her face and scanned down the list. "How will I figure out who the ghost is?"

"I might be able to find some photos of some of the keepers." Anton tapped his chin with his index finger. "I'll head to the historical society later this afternoon." Eyeing Lin, he said, "You might want to go back to the lighthouse. Obviously, this ghost wants something from you. He wouldn't have materialized if he didn't."

"I'll have to go back when the work crews are finished for the day. I don't want people asking questions about why I'm out there visiting."

Anton gave a shrug. "That's simple to explain. Your boyfriend is out there working on the renovations."

"It would be odd if I just show up. I hardly ever visit Jeff when he's on a project, and besides, I have to work." Lin glanced up at the kitchen wall clock. "Speaking of which, I'd better get to my first client."

Nicky roused himself when he heard Lin moving around the kitchen and then followed her towards the back door.

"I'll let you know what I find at the historical

museum." Anton walked Lin to the door.

Lin thanked the man for his help and headed to her truck that was parked at the curb in front of the house. She opened the truck door to let Nicky into the passenger seat and then she got in and drove towards the island town of 'Sconset to the day's first landscaping customer. Her window was down and warm, fresh air blew into the car causing strands of her hair to float around her head. Nicky lifted his snoot and sniffed the breeze.

Lin's thoughts focused on the new ghost wondering why he'd revealed himself and what he might need from her. Strong feelings had emanated from the spirit and had filled Lin's heart with a sadness so heavy it was almost crushing. She didn't look forward to seeing the man again and she let out an audible sigh that caused Nicky to turn to her and whine.

Smiling at her little rescue dog's concern, Lin said, "It's okay, Nick. I'm okay."

Once they arrived at the enormous estate, Lin worked for two hours under the warm sun mowing, weeding, and replacing the spent flowers in the garden's beds with new ones. Admiring the wide, green lawns and the beautiful landscaping, she plopped back on her butt, wiping some sweat from her brow when a text from Jeff came in.

Can you meet me at the lighthouse for lunch? I need to talk to you.

Lin's heart started to race wondering what was so important that Jeff asked her to come to the work site in the middle of the day. Checking her watch, she jumped to her feet, called to the dog, and then hurried off to the next three clients on her list in order to finish in time to meet Jeff at the lighthouse.

***

Jeff was waiting at the gravel driveway when Lin pulled the truck to a stop. Nicky spotted the man, let out a bark of excitement, and wagged his little tail waiting impatiently for his owner to let him out of the vehicle.

Lin hugged Jeff and the dog danced around them, delighted to see the carpenter in the middle of the work-day. Jeff bent and greeted the friendly creature and when he stood up, Lin could see the lines of worry creasing his forehead.

"What's wrong?" Lin asked.

Jeff took he girlfriend's arm and directed her away from the small parking lot to the bluff overlooking the ocean. "One of the guys got hurt today." Running his hand over his head, Jeff paused to collect himself.

"What happened?" As she'd driven up the hill to the lighthouse, Lin had experienced a growing sense of dread and alarm, and now she knew why.

"The scaffolding went up in the barn the other day." Jeff's face was pale. "It was checked by two guys. This morning, one of the workers went up there. He was on the platform for about a minute when we all heard a creaking sound. It got louder and then one of the cross pieces that make up the floor tumbled to the ground. Dave was up there, he was grabbing at anything he could to hold on to, but the floor he was standing on crashed down."

Lin held her breath. "Is Dave...?"

"He's hurt pretty bad." Jeff rubbed at the side of his face. "The ambulance came, took him to the hospital. He's been airlifted to Boston, to General Hospital."

Lin let out a long breath. "Oh, no."

"Kurt's business has never had an accident like this. He's all about safety, even if it costs him money. The workers are the number one priority. Kurt went with Dave in the ambulance and in the helicopter to Boston."

"Kurt's a good guy." Lin turned and looked towards the barn.

"Some police officers and an investigator are inside the barn checking everything out. All the guys have been sent home for the rest of the day."

"Does anyone know what happened?" Lin asked. "Why did it fall?"

Jeff waited for Lin to turn back to him. "Some of the bolts were loose." He looked at her pointedly.

23

"Those bolts were tight yesterday."

"Someone tampered with them?" Lin kept her voice down even though no one was nearby.

"That's what we think."

Lin noticed that Nicky had wandered down to the lighthouse, but when she called for him to return, he didn't budge. "Nick!"

The dog didn't even look back at his owner, he just stood transfixed staring at the door at the base of the lighthouse.

Lin groaned and started down the path, but then she halted abruptly. "He always comes when I call him, unless...." Lin's voice trailed off.

A look of alarm passed over Jeff's face as he took Lin's hand and the two descended the slight hill to the lighthouse. The dog had gone behind the structure so Lin and Jeff walked around to the other side to see what the canine was up to.

"Do you feel anything?" Jeff questioned Lin.

She shook her head. "Where has that dog gone?" Lin grumped as she stepped around the base circling the lighthouse with Jeff following close behind.

When they reached the side near the keeper's house, Lin put her hands on her hips and turned, her eyes searching in every direction. A sudden, terrible feeling of anxiety washed over her, and she rushed to one of the windows of the old house to peer inside. The sun's reflection on the glass made it hard to see into the rooms and Lin raised her hand like a hat's visor to shield her eyes.

"I think Nicky's inside," Lin said in a quavering voice.

She and Jeff darted from window to window looking into the small rooms of the cottage until Jeff shouted from the opposite side and Lin ran to him.

"He's here." Jeff pointed through the window.

Lin stood on tip-toes to get a look. "What's he doing in there?"

The little brown dog was curled up on an old, tattered rug next to a dirty rocking chair in front of the small, stone fireplace. When Lin realized that the chair was rocking gently back and forth, she wondered why she didn't feel the familiar gust of cold air envelop her. "Jeff, the chair is rocking on its own."

Jeff's eyes widened as he turned to his girlfriend, concern etched over his face.

Watching for a few more moments to see if anyone materialized, Lin knocked on the glass. "Nick." Her voice was almost a whisper.

The dog lifted his head and glanced up to the window.

"Nick, come out of there. Come on, right now."

The dog took a long look at the rocking chair and then slowly rose from his resting position. He trotted out of the cottage's living area and into the space that had once served as the kitchen. In a few seconds, he came bounding around from the front of the house, wagging his stub of a tail.

Lin felt like scolding the happy creature, but she couldn't bring herself to do it. "If you can't behave, I'll bring a leash next time so we don't have any disappearing dogs."

"What about the rocking?" Jeff followed Lin as she stepped away from the house.

"Maybe it was just a breeze that was making it move." Lin didn't believe her statement and knew Jeff probably didn't either. She looked over her shoulder to the keeper's cottage. "Do you think I should see if I can pick up on anything around the grounds? Maybe I should try and sense what's going on."

Jeff nodded. "I thought since the guys were gone and the accident had just happened this morning, you might be able to pick up on ... whatever?"

"I'll try. Let's walk around."

The dog stayed with Lin and Jeff as they made the rounds near the property's three structures and then they spent time wandering along the bluff and the grassy areas of the space.

"I'm not picking up on anything. I can't feel a thing." Lin tipped her head back to look up to the top of the lighthouse. "I don't see anything either."

"Why won't he show himself?" Jeff asked.

Giving a shrug, Lin sighed. "I don't know anything about ghosts. I only see them."

After a few more minutes, the two decided to part ways since Lin still had several gardens to tend before the day was over.

"I'm sorry I was no help."

Jeff hugged her. "I'm upset over what happened here this morning. It made me feel better to talk to you."

Driving towards her next client's home, Lin thought about why the ghost hadn't appeared and wondered if he was the one responsible for the accident at the barn. *Maybe I didn't see a ghost the other day at all. Maybe it was just some shadowy reflection in the lighthouse glass and I only imagined someone was up there.*

The rocking of the keeper's house chair popped into Lin's mind. *Maybe it* was *just the breeze causing the chair to move.*

Lin sighed and gripped the steering wheel as she shook her head from side to side. There was just no way to ignore the facts.

There is definitely a ghost.

CHAPTER 4

Lin marked out the new garden bed that was going in behind her client's antique Colonial home while waiting for her landscaping partner to arrive. Nicky heard the man's approach and darted across the lush green lawn to greet him. In his early sixties, Leonard was tall and tanned, and although he was slender, his arms and shoulders were muscular from years of outside work.

"Did it go okay?" Lin started towards her partner. "How do you feel?"

"As bad as I look." Leonard raised his hand and placed two fingers gingerly against his cheek on the side where he had just had a root canal. "I don't know why I listened to you."

"I never thought you'd actually go." Lin lifted the heavy bag of tools from the man's hand.

"I had to go," Leonard growled. "If I didn't go, your nagging about it would never have ended."

All summer, Lin had been encouraging Leonard to visit a dentist to have work done on his teeth.

Two of his back molars had been aching, he had two missing teeth, and some others were crooked and twisted in the gum. "It's better for your health," she told him every time he complained about a tooth hurting. "If you get them fixed," she'd said, "then you'll be even more handsome than you already are. All the women will be after you."

Leonard had grunted when he'd heard that. "I'm not interested. I'm never getting married again. I told you that."

Lin narrowed her eyes at the man, but she held her tongue. She guessed that Leonard's late wife, Marguerite, wouldn't have wanted him to be alone.

Leonard took a look at the work Lin had started and then sank onto the grass in the shade of a big Maple tree. "What you've done looks good." Leaning against the trunk of the tree he added, "The dentist told me that I couldn't exert myself until tomorrow so it seems you'll be the one doing all the heavy lifting today."

Lin stared at him with her hand on her hip and grumped. "Maybe it wasn't such a good idea to encourage you to have your teeth done."

From his comfortable spot on the grass, Leonard offered suggestions and gave a few instructions as he and Nicky sat together watching Lin work in the hot sun. After an hour, Lin brought her lunch bag over and joined them in the shade. "I made you some custard." She handed the man a container. "I thought you'd need something soft to eat."

Leonard took it gratefully. "I'm starving. Thanks, Coffin."

Handing Nicky a dog treat, Lin wiped the sweat off her brow with the back of her hand and bit into her sandwich. She told Leonard about the work Jeff was doing at the East End Lighthouse and about the odd and dangerous happenings that had been going on.

Leonard's brow furrowed. "They need to get to the bottom of that. Someone tampered with the equipment, caused an accident? They've got a troubled person on that crew."

"You think it's someone on the crew?" Lin asked. "Jeff and I wondered if it could be someone outside of the crew, a tourist or an island resident might be sneaking around at night causing the trouble."

Leonard shook his head slowly. "I don't know about that. It's possible, I suppose. I might put my money on one of the workers."

"Would you? That's pretty awful not to be able to trust your own co-workers."

"Exactly." Leonard spooned some custard into his mouth.

"What do you mean? Why do you say that?" Lin offered the dog a piece of her sandwich and he took it gently from her hand.

"There are two reasons for someone to cause trouble." Leonard poked the air with the spoon for emphasis. "One, the person is mentally unstable and just wants to hurt others. The second reason would be to disrupt the project. I'd lean towards someone wanting to stop the renovation work."

"Why would someone want that to happen?" Lin tilted her head.

Shrugging, Leonard said, "Some sort of gain."

"Like what? It isn't private property. That land hasn't been in private hands for almost two hundred years. How could someone gain from disrupting the process?"

Leonard made eye contact with Lin. "When you find out what the gain might be, then you'll know who to focus your suspicions on."

Lin's mind whirred thinking about how a person might profit from stopping the lighthouse project and she came up empty ... except for the ghost. Maybe he wanted to keep the workers away because they were a nuisance to his peace and quiet. Even though a few visitors appeared at the lighthouse on a daily basis, they weren't traipsing around inside the buildings and they didn't stay that long. The spirit man might not appreciate the work team interfering with his privacy.

"Any ideas?" Leonard asked.

"Huh?" Leonard's question pulled Lin from her thoughts and she shook herself slightly. "No. I can't come up with any ideas about how someone could profit from disrupting the workers." *Except for the ghost.*

Leonard stared at his partner suspiciously. "Not a single idea? None at all?"

"None," Lin repeated. "I'd tell you if I thought of anything. Can you think of anything?"

"Is there any more custard?" Leonard leaned over to look into Lin's lunch container.

Smiling, Lin replied, "I made a whole custard pie for you. It's in the cooler in my truck."

"An angel from heaven." Leonard attempted a grin, but winced from the pain in his mouth. "I should never have gone to that darned dentist."

"It will feel better soon," Lin said reassuringly. "You've lived on the island forever. What could there be about the lighthouse that would make someone want the workers to clear out of there?"

Leonard adjusted his back against the tree and looked off across the yard. "I'd have to give that some thought."

"I asked Anton about it, too. He's going to look into the history of the light and find out about the keepers."

Leonard gave Lin a look. "What's the historian think he's going to find? The keepers are long dead. What's the point of reading about the keepers?"

Lin could have kicked herself for mentioning that Anton was researching the lighthouse keepers. Leonard didn't know anything about Lin's ability to see ghosts and she had to think fast to cover the real reason Anton was looking for information. "Anton is trying to see if there's a mystery about the lighthouse that someone might know. If there's a mystery of some kind, then that could be the reason that someone would want the workers out of there."

"Well, good luck to him. I don't think he's going to find the answer to these troubles in a book."

"Where do you think we'll find the answer?" Lin scooted around on the grass so she could face Leonard.

"I might start by looking at the guys working the job."

Lin's eyes widened. "You really think one of them is responsible?"

Nicky rolled over so that Leonard could rub his belly and the man obliged. "What's the makeup of the group? Do these guys always work together? Are there newcomers to the crew?"

"I don't know. I'll have to ask Jeff about it."

"I'll ask around, find out if there's anyone I know working on the project."

"That would be great. The more information we can gather, the better." Lin nodded just as her cell phone buzzed. "It's a text from Jeff. He says that what happened today has been deemed an accident. The crew can go back to work tomorrow." Looking up from the phone, Lin blew out a long sigh as her heart raced with concern. "I'm worried. Jeff was so excited about working on this project. Right now,

I'd do anything to get him to leave that job."

"Jeff's a smart guy, Coffin. He'll be okay." Leonard touched his swollen cheek. "This thing's killing me. I think I'm going to head home. You okay finishing this garden bed on your own?"

Lin teased, "You haven't actually been a whole lot of help to me today. I think I can handle it." She gave her partner a playful poke on his arm and then stood up. "Come on, let's go to my truck. I'll give you that custard pie."

"Thanks, Coffin."

Lin removed the pie from the cooler and handed it to Leonard. As he headed to his own truck carrying the custard, he turned back to Lin. "Be sure to tell Jeff to keep his eyes open. Tell him to stay safe."

Giving a nod, Lin watched her partner climb into his truck and drive away and just as she was about to return to the yard to finish the garden work, a gust of cold air blew over her causing the little hairs on her arms to stand up. She froze in place.

Taking in a deep breath, she started to turn to look behind her expecting to see the ghost standing a few yards away. Pivoting slowly on her heel, Lin was surprised at what she saw.

The yard was empty. There wasn't a ghost in sight.

CHAPTER 5

"And then I got that ice cold feeling of being in a walk-in freezer so I turned around expecting the ghost. Guess what I saw?" Lin sat with her cousin at a small café table near the beverage and dessert counter at the back of Viv's bookstore.

Viv put her cookie on the plate in front of her. "The ghost, of course."

Lin paused for emphasis. "Nothing. I didn't see anything because the ghost wasn't there."

"Did you feel cold from the breeze? Was it a false alarm?"

"I'm sure it was a spirit that caused the sensation. When the cold comes over me, it always feels a little different than something caused by the weather. I can tell the difference now. It was definitely from a ghost."

With a look of concern on her face, Viv shifted in her seat as she glanced around to see who was nearby. Lowering her voice, she asked, "Why won't the ghost materialize? This has never happened before. You feel that he's near you, but he doesn't show himself? What does it mean?"

Lin's eyebrow went up. "I don't think it means anything. I think the ghost might just be shy or reserved."

Viv didn't take her eyes off her cousin's face.

"Why are you looking at me like that?"

"Because," Viv leaned forward, "this ghost might be malicious. You could always see the other ghosts that you've dealt with. They materialized. This one doesn't. Is he stalking you?"

Lin leaned back against her seat with a start. "Stalking me? Why would he?"

"There have been several times when you've sensed he's been around you, but he stays invisible. You sensed him in the rocking chair at the keeper's house and yesterday you thought he was behind you at your client's home. There was another time, too." Viv pressed her finger against her temple. "This ghost is probably responsible for the trouble at the lighthouse project." Shaking her head, she muttered, "I don't like it. Not one bit. What's wrong with him? What does he want from you?"

Lin held her hands up in a helpless gesture.

"If he wants something, then he'd better become visible." Viv gave a grunt of disgust and then an expression of panic washed over her face. "Do you think he can hear me? I don't want to get him angry. Well, he must be angry already if he's causing trouble at the lighthouse. I just mean I don't want him angry *with me*. I don't want a stalker following *me* around."

Lin reminded her cousin. "You can't see ghosts, Viv. You would never know if he was stalking you."

"You know what I mean." Viv waved her hand around. "Have you heard anything from Anton?"

"Not yet." Lin glanced over at Nicky snoozing in the easy chair cuddled next to Queenie. "I wish I could curl up in a chair with my crossword books and forget all about this trouble."

"How's the guy who got hurt at the lighthouse? Have you heard any updates?" Viv asked.

"Jeff told me that Dave is going to be okay. He's got a few broken bones and there was some internal bleeding, but it's stopped now. He'll need a long recovery period."

"Thank heavens he's going to be fine." Viv nodded. "Jeff needs to be careful out there."

"Don't I know it. Worry is always picking at the back of my mind." Lin reached up and nervously fiddled with a strand of her long brown hair.

Placing her elbow on the table, Viv rested her chin in her hand. "What do *you* think is going on? Is the ghost causing the trouble at the work site or is it a living person who's doing the sabotaging?"

"I don't know what to think." Lin gave a slight shrug of her shoulder. "I wish I knew."

"I really hope it's not the ghost who's

responsible." A frown pulled the corners of Viv's mouth down. "That scares me to death. How do you catch a ghost? How do you stop him from his wickedness? You can't put him in handcuffs. You can't arrest him. You can't put him in jail."

The cousins stared at each other.

Viv asked again, "If the ghost is the guilty party, then how on earth do you stop him?"

Lin shifted her gaze across the bookstore moving her eyes from the polished wood of the dessert and beverage bar to the shelves lined with hardcovers and paperbacks, over the comfortable chairs and sofas, the glossy hardwood floors, the old tin ceiling, to the customers peacefully browsing and reading. "I need to find out what is causing his upset. I need to find out why he's so angry." Looking back at Viv, Lin said, "I need to find out how I can help him. Then, he'll stop."

"Are you sure he'll stop?"

Hesitating for a moment, Lin said softly, "Pretty sure."

With the long strap of a black leather briefcase laying over his shoulder, Anton Wilson raced around one of the bookshelves and over to Lin and Viv's table where he took a seat. "I knew I'd find you here." He rested the briefcase bulging with papers and books on the floor between his feet.

"Speak of the devil." Viv smiled at the slightly disheveled historian. "I asked Lin if she'd heard from you, and here you are."

Anton pulled some books and notebooks from his bag. "The lighthouse information is always fascinating to me." The man looked across the room through the lenses of his eyeglasses. "I'm drawn to the idea of being a keeper, providing safety to travelers via the light. It appeals to my sense of order, of making things right in the world." He let out a sigh. "It wouldn't suit me though. I'm not one for being outside or withstanding the elements to keep the light working properly. Perhaps in my next life, I will be more robust."

Lin and Viv chuckled at Anton's musings.

"You have a robust mind, Anton," Lin told him with a smile. "Which has helped bring order to many of the mysteries we've worked on."

Anton sat straighter in his chair and his eyes twinkled. "You're right. In my own way, I am very much like a keeper of a lighthouse."

Viv brought the topic of conversation to the most recent of mysteries. "Did you find anything helpful?"

"Possibly." Anton flipped through the pages of one of his books and when he found what he wanted, he placed the book on the table and slid it over to Lin. "Here are a few pictures of some of the later lighthouse keepers. Do any of them look familiar?"

Lin pulled the book closer and leaned forward to

peer at the six photographs on the page. Shaking her head, she looked up. "No. None of these men is the person I saw at the light."

Viv's eyes went wide. "Wait a minute. How do we know that the ghost you saw is a former keeper? It could be any ghost, just hanging out there."

Lin stared at her cousin. "I hadn't thought of that possibility." Turning the pages of Anton's book and reading the captions under photos of the lighthouses, Lin said, "I don't know. I might be wrong, but I get the feeling the spirit I saw was once a keeper."

"Have you seen him recently?" Anton questioned.

"I haven't, no."

"Maybe he's gone," Anton offered.

Viv rolled her eyes. "That would be a blessing, but I don't think he's gone anywhere. Lin feels the cold, but he doesn't show up. He stays invisible. I think he's a stalker."

"What would the ghost gain by stalking Lin?" Anton took the book off the table and packed it into his briefcase. "I've been reading about the different keepers. Some have more information published about them than others do. Three stood out to me. One of them met with a tragic accident."

A chill ran through Lin's body as she gave Anton her full attention waiting to hear the details.

"You know the lighthouse used to be closer to

the bluff? Erosion wore away at the cliff and the lighthouse had to moved back from the edge. Anyway, during a storm before it was moved, the keeper fell from the cliff to the rocks below and was killed."

Lin groaned as pricks of worry picked at her skin. "What was his name?"

Anton looked down at his notes. "Jackson Best." Raising his eyes to the cousins, he added, "Some people think the fall was self-inflicted." Anton looked pointedly at the two young women.

"You mean he jumped?" Viv put her hand to her throat, imagining tumbling from the steep cliffs at East End. "Oh, how terrible."

"Why do people think he jumped?" Lin nervously pushed her hair back from her face. "Was there something the man was despondent over?"

"I have yet to find that information." Anton buried his nose in his notes. "Here's the next one. Nathaniel Mathers. He was keeper in the mid-1850s and held the position for six years."

The two young women leaned forward waiting for the information.

"I think he could be your ghost because," Anton looked over the rims of his eyeglasses at Lin, "it seems the man went off the deep end during his final years at the lighthouse."

"What does that mean?" Viv wrinkled her nose.

"It seems Mr. Mathers lost touch with reality. He stopped eating, was often found up in the light rocking back and forth, muttering."

"What was he muttering about?" Lin wondered if she really wanted to know the answer.

"The account I read didn't mention what the man was babbling about." Anton's face was serious. "Of course, Mr. Mathers was removed from his position."

"This is depressing," Lin frowned. "Does that lighthouse have a curse on it?"

Viv eyed her cousin. "A curse? We're going from bad to worse here."

Feeling oddly dizzy, Lin steeled herself to hear about the next lighthouse keeper who could be the new ghost. "You said there were three possible candidates for my ghost."

"Yes. The final possibility is Benjamin Day. Day was named keeper after Mr. Mathers was removed from the job and right before Jackson Best took over. When his wife passed away, Mr. Day fell into sadness and could not shake it off. Reports indicate that he never recovered his zest for life."

Viv turned to look at Lin. "Do you feel anything when Anton mentions their names? Does one person in particular give you a funny feeling?"

"They all do," Lin moaned. "Their circumstances are horrible. The ghost could be any of those men."

Viv stood up. "I have to get back to work. We

need a break from all of this. I'm glad we're going to Bakerback tomorrow."

The following day, Lin, Jeff, Viv, and John had plans to kayak over to the small island of Bakerback off the coast of Nantucket. As soon as Viv mentioned the kayaking trip, a sense of anxiety gripped Lin like a vise and her heart sank. A thought ran through her mind.

The kayaking outing might not be the break that we're hoping for.

CHAPTER 6

After leaving the bookstore and with her little dog trotting along beside, Lin walked up the brick sidewalks on her way to her cottage carrying two books lent to her by Anton. A text from Jeff arrived telling her that the work day at the lighthouse had passed without incident and Lin let out a long sigh of relief. Every time she received a text from Jeff during the day, her heart jumped into her throat from worry that something might have happened to her boyfriend.

"Jeff's safe, Nick," Lin said to her dog. "Nothing happened at the lighthouse today."

The little brown creature looked up at his owner and let out a happy woof.

Once inside the gray-shingled home, Lin placed the books on the kitchen island and she ran her fingertip over the hardbound cover of one of the history volumes. Her hand could feel a low-level buzz of energy emanating from the book.

As she boiled a few eggs, made some rice, and

prepared a green salad, Lin's eyes kept darting over to the book and each time, a flicker of nervousness skittered over her skin. She settled at the deck table with her dinner and taking a first bite, Lin opened the cover of the history book and turned some of the pages until she found the place where Anton had shown her photographs of some of the lighthouse keepers.

Peering at the pictures, Lin read the names of each keeper printed underneath the photos. The three men that Anton thought might be the lighthouse's ghost stared back at Lin from the photographs and drawings and she turned her eyes from one to the other and then back again. The pictures gave off such a strong vibrating energy that Lin wouldn't have been surprised if the men started to move within the photographic frames or if they spoke to her from the page.

"Which one of you is the ghost?" Lin whispered. The men looked similar to one another and either one could be the spirit she'd seen high in the lighthouse.

She was so engrossed in the book that she didn't notice how dark it had become until a cool breeze brushed over her bare arms and caused her to shiver. She rubbed her limbs and looked around for the dog. "Nick?"

Lin gathered the history books and her empty dinner plate and headed into the kitchen where she found her sweet creature curled up sound asleep in the corner on his doggy bed. Lifting his head, Nicky blinked sleepily at his owner and then his expression changed as he jumped to his feet and turned his head towards the deck. The speed and urgency of the dog's movement made Lin's stomach muscles clench.

"What's wrong, Nick?" Lin kept her voice soft as she gripped the edge of the counter and followed his gaze through the glass doors to the deck. Moving her feet over the wood floor, she flicked the wall switch to turn the kitchen lights off so she could better see into the yard ... and if someone was outside, it would make it harder for him to see her.

Suddenly, Jeff came around the corner of the house and stepped up onto the deck. He waved to his girlfriend as he moved to the door and Lin unlocked it for him.

Entering the kitchen, he pulled Lin into a hug. "I thought I heard you out on the deck so I came around to the back. It must have been the wind or something that I heard."

"We were on the deck, but we just came in."

Jeff had a brown paper bag in one hand. "I brought dessert. It's whoopee pies."

A smile spread over Lin's face and she moaned. "I love whoopee pies." She took Jeff's hand and led him to the kitchen table where he opened the bag and removed a small bakery box. Lin went to the cabinets, lifted small pale blue plates from the shelves, and took silver forks from the drawer. She took a few glances to the outside wondering what Jeff had heard in the backyard that made him think that Lin was on the deck.

Jeff picked up on Lin's unease. "What's wrong?"

Lin waved her hand around. "Oh, nothing. I've just been on edge today." She made tea and carried the mugs to the table. "Tell me how the work went at the lighthouse."

They settled in their seats and Jeff placed a whoopee pie on each of their plates and the two dug into the sweets. "The day went smoothly. Everyone was watchful though. The workers don't know who they can trust ... or not trust. It's a bigger crew. We don't know some of the guys that well so there's some uneasiness. The work isn't moving along as smoothly as it would if the whole crew had been working together for a while, but it's okay."

"Nothing was amiss? Nothing seemed out of the ordinary?"

Jeff wiped some of the cream filling from his lips. "Nothing went wrong. Thankfully, no one got hurt today."

"Thank heavens." Lin took a sip of her tea. "I'd be nervous all day long if I was working there."

Jeff's eyes widened. "Oh, that reminds me. Kurt asked if you'd like to do the landscaping for the project."

Lin had to swallow hard to loosen the tightness she felt in her throat. "Did he?"

Eyeing Lin, Jeff said, "I can hear the hesitation in your voice."

Lin's lips turned up. "Am I that transparent?"

"Don't take the project if it makes you anxious. You and Leonard have plenty of work."

Lin rubbed the side of her face. "Normally, I'd jump at the chance to work at the lighthouse. It's just...." She let her voice trail off.

"I think there are a number of guys who wish they hadn't signed up for this job. We're all worried that some form of sabotage will happen again. If you aren't comfortable working at the lighthouse, then just say no."

Lin's shoulders drooped and a loud sigh escaped her lungs. "I need to give it some thought."

"I'll tell Kurt that you're thinking it over." Jeff took a second whoopee pie from the bakery box.

"I'd like to talk to Leonard about working there. I wouldn't want to put him at any risk." Lin lifted a bite of the dessert to her mouth. "Were all the workers present today at the lighthouse? Was anyone off for the day?"

Jeff swallowed and didn't answer right away, thinking it over. "You know, I'm not sure." He realized that someone taking the day off might be the reason that nothing had happened at the work site. Jeff leveled his eyes at Lin. "Have you seen any ghosts lately?"

Lin shook her head. "I don't know why the ghost appeared in the lighthouse that day we were there. If he wants something, then why show up once and not again? How will I figure out what he wants from me if he remains invisible?"

"Could it just be that he wanted to acknowledge you because he knew you could see him? Maybe he doesn't want anything at all."

"That hasn't happened before with the ghosts I've seen on the island, but I suppose it's a possibility." Lin placed her fork on her dessert plate and crossed her arms leaning on the table. "The whole thing has been making me very uneasy." Lin showed Jeff the books that Anton lent to her and opened one of them so that he could see the three men who'd worked as keepers. "Anton suggested that one of these men could be the lighthouse ghost."

Jeff read the short passages about the men and studied their pictures. When he lifted his head, he asked, "Do you get a sense that one of them is your ghost?"

"Maybe. I could feel some energy coming off one picture in particular." She pointed to the photo and when she touched it, little zips of electricity jumped at her fingers. "I can feel it now."

"Benjamin Day," Jeff read. "His wife passed away. Why would he be causing trouble at the lighthouse?"

Lin shrugged. "I have no idea. If he wants help with something, then he'd better show up so I can figure it out."

Jeff and Lin chatted for another thirty minutes until both were yawning from their work-week of early morning risings so Jeff kissed his girlfriend goodnight and left for his own house. "I'll see you at the docks bright and early tomorrow."

Jeff's words caused a wave of anxiety to wash over Lin and she shook herself as she cleared the kitchen table and put the plates and mugs in the dishwasher. She'd been looking forward to their outing to Bakerback Island, but every time it had come up in conversation that day, she'd become worried and nervous.

Lin turned the switch to light up the deck and asked Nicky if he wanted to go outside one last time before she locked the doggy door and headed to bed. Nicky stretched and yawned and Lin opened the glass door so he could climb down the few steps and head into the backyard. She followed the dog out to the deck to pick up the silverware she'd left on the table from dinner.

As she reached for the fork and knife, the dog let out a high-pitched whine that caused Lin's blood to freeze. A whoosh of icy air engulfed her and she slowly turned around expecting to see the ghost from the lighthouse. The silverware dropped from her grasp and clattered to the deck floor when she saw the figure standing on the patio.

A pale ghost woman, drenched, water puddling on the patio stones, reached out to Lin with a trembling hand. Tears poured from her eyes and some strands of her soaking wet hair stuck to her cheeks. A rush of wind whipped around Lin causing her own hair to blow back from her face and a terrible, mournful wailing sound made Lin's heart clench with sadness. Lin wasn't sure if the sound had come from the sudden gust rushing through the leaves or from the spirit standing a few yards away.

Opening her mouth to speak, the ghost's form became more and more transparent until she disappeared into the night air.

"No, don't go," Lin called, but it was too late.

Shivering and overcome by the heaviness of grief flowing from the ghost, Lin sank onto the deck floor as Nicky darted to her side. Wrapping her arms around the sweet creature, Lin put her face against the dog's soft fur and tears fell from her eyes.

CHAPTER 7

"Lin feels like she might be coming down with a cold," Viv told John. "Let's just take your boat over to Bakerback and then we'll launch the kayaks from there. It will be less strenuous than kayaking all the way over." Viv lifted the picnic basket she had in her hand. "I made a nice lunch for us. When we get to the island, we can drop anchor and eat lunch on the boat. Taking your boat over will give us more time to walk around the trails, kayak, and swim." Smiling at her boyfriend, Viv said, "It's a much better idea than kayaking all that way."

"Fine with me." John eyed Lin. "You okay? You sure you want to go?"

Lin nodded. "I've been looking forward to it."

Last night, after the ghost woman made her appearance, Lin had called Viv and the young woman rushed over to listen to what had happened. She ended up staying for two hours to talk with and comfort her cousin. When Viv heard Lin's reservations about the kayaking trip the next day, she blanched with concern. "Just to be on the safe side, we'll change our plans. It's a long trip in the kayaks. I'd feel better if we take the boat. We can kayak around once we cross over to the island."

When John dropped anchor, Viv bustled around heating the lunch in the galley while Lin and Jeff set the deck table and then helped John launch and tie off the kayaks so they would be ready to go. John carried iced tea, fresh-squeezed orange juice, and lemonade to the table along with a platter of appetizers. "I think this *was* a better idea." He nodded to Lin with a grin as he poured iced tea and lemonade into his glass. "We can relax for a while before we head out with the kayaks."

They sat around the table in the shade under the canvas overhang and dug into the delicious lunch that Viv had prepared. Passing around the dishes of Swedish meatballs, egg noodles with gravy, homemade rolls, tomato, green bean and onion salad, and garlic and lemon broccolini, Jeff chuckled and said, "I think we would have sunk if we'd eaten all this food before trying to kayak over from Nantucket."

Viv told the others, "I brought some cookies and chocolate-coffee squares from the bookstore café so leave some room for dessert."

After the meal, the four sunned themselves on the deck, each one nearly nodding off from the gentle rocking of the boat.

With closed eyes and his hands folded across his chest, Jeff told John, "It's a good thing I don't live on a boat like you do. I'd just nap all the time and never get anything done."

The group roused themselves from a forty-minute snooze, changed into swimsuits, and lowered themselves into the kayaks. Viv almost tumbled out of hers as she gingerly maneuvered into it and she let out shrieks as the kayak swayed violently from side to side until she finally managed to settle. "Not a great start," Viv pushed her golden brown hair from her eyes with one hand and clutched the paddle with the other. When everyone was safely sitting, the guys led the way to Bakerback with Lin and Viv paddling along next to each other.

"It's a beautiful day." Taking brisk strokes with her paddle, Lin looked up at the bright blue sky just as a flock of small birds flew so closely overhead that Viv's instinct caused her to duck.

"Sheesh." Viv laughed.

For an hour, the four young people moved at a quick pace gracefully over the water until Viv called out the need for a rest and they beached the kayaks and stepped onto the soft, white beach. Viv stretched back on the warm sand while her three companions jumped into the turquoise water and swam and body-surfed in the swells of the refreshing ocean. Even though she was enjoying the outing, Lin couldn't help taking glances over her shoulder every few minutes looking for a ghost.

After the swimmers dried off in the sun, the four young people pulled t-shirts and shorts over their swimsuits, dried their feet with towels, and put their athletic shoes on to head off along the nature trails that covered the small island.

Bakerback, a six-hundred-acre island off the coast of Nantucket, was privately owned by its residents and had no paved roads or public utilities. Water was provided by wells and electricity came from solar energy or gas-powered generators. Covered with beach grass, rosa rugosa, scrub oak, bayberry, red maple, and beach plum, the island was home to piping plovers, owls, terns, and harbor and gray seals. A few day-visitors were tolerated by the residents and Lin, Viv, and the guys respected the island and its inhabitants by not staying long and not visiting often.

"Have you seen anyone? Any ghosts around?" Viv whispered to her cousin as they hiked along.

"Nothing. But I'm looking over my shoulder all the time."

Viv gave a nod. "Let me know if anyone ... appears."

"You'll know just by looking at me," Lin groaned.

Climbing to the top of a small hill and enjoying the gorgeous eastern view of the island, the ocean, and Nantucket in the distance, the foursome rounded the last bend and came out from a grove of pine trees to see a wall of black clouds heading towards them from the west.

"This wasn't predicted." John stood staring at the approaching storm. The sun was still shining over them, but it wouldn't be long before the dark clouds overtook the area.

"What should we do?" Viv's voice shook when she saw flashes of lightning zapping between the clouds in the distance.

"You think we have time to get back to the boat?" Lin asked. "We could shelter on board until it blows over."

"I'm not sure. Depends on how strong this thing is." John pulled out his phone to check the Coast Guard website. "The anchor might not hold if it's a bad one."

"We might need to take the chance." Jeff looked at Lin. "I think we should do what you suggested and get back to the boat."

"Whatever we do, we better do it fast." Viv wrapped her arms around herself.

They took off running down the hill and over the trails that led back to the shore with the wind whipping up and raindrops starting to fall. By the time they reached the beach, the sun had been obliterated by the angry, black clouds and the four were drenched from the pelting rain.

"Didn't we leave the kayaks right here?" John shouted to his companions over the blowing wind.

Pushing her wet hair out of her eyes, Lin turned in a circle trying to locate the kayaks when last night's visit from the ghost popped into her mind and caused her to shudder. The heavy wind wailed like the awful sound she heard last night when the spirit showed up on her patio. Lin and her friends were soaked through just like the ghost-woman.

Jogging east along the beach and unable to find the kayaks, they reversed direction and ran into the rain and wind with the hopes of seeing the kayaks somewhere near the shore. Viv stopped and hunched over, wheezing. She shouted, "They're gone, and anyway, it's too dangerous now. We can't use them to get to the boat."

A blast of thunder and a blinding flash of lightning made Lin jump. "We need to find shelter!"

"We can move into the scrub and lie down flat on the ground." Jeff pointed to the dunes and brush and they rushed in that direction just as a crash from the lightning rocked the beach with such force that the foursome stumbled.

Viv clutched John's arm and began to cry. "It's too dangerous. We'll be struck by lightning. What are we going to do?"

Lin's heart pounded like a bass drum as she turned, searching desperately for somewhere to shelter. A sudden whoosh of freezing air surrounded her causing her entire soaking wet body to shake violently. Blinking hard against the rain, Lin's gaze was drawn across the dune and there, near the bottom of the hill, stood the ghost woman, her hand outstretched to Lin.

Lin bolted towards the spirit with her three friends running after her. The ghost turned and Lin followed her over the dunes struggling hard to move her feet over the drenched sand. The woman stood, her body glimmering like a beacon at the edge of a group of maple trees, and Lin watched as the ghost's atoms swirled for a few seconds and disappeared. Breathing hard, Lin leaned forward with her hands on her thighs when she heard Jeff shout.

"There's a shack."

The four stumbled to the small structure and flung the unlocked door open. They sank to the floor sucking in deep breaths, dripping wet and shivering. As the brunt of the storm thundered around them, the lightning crashed outside the small hut that someone had made to store surf boards.

"Thank heavens we're out of that storm," Viv squeezed her cousin's arm.

"That was a stroke a luck." John had to raise his voice over the din outside. "How did you ever see this thing through all the rain?"

Hugging her knees tucked up close to her body, Lin lifted her head from her arms. "I don't know," she mumbled, still shaking from the cold that had engulfed her. Though she couldn't tell John that a ghost had led them to the surfer's hut, Lin made eye contact with Jeff and then Viv, and the looks on their faces told her that they knew how she'd found the shack. Questions swirled in Lin's brain.

Who is that ghost? What is going on?

CHAPTER 8

When the storm finally let up, the friends walked the sandy shoreline and found two of their kayaks, one floating a few yards out in the ocean and the other one flipped over and beached. Viv and John rode together and Lin and Jeff sat in the second kayak as the four slowly made their way to John's boat, thankfully still tethered to its anchor. There was little conversation on the short trip back to Nantucket, the four of them still feeling shaken from the misadventure on Bakerback Island.

"I've never seen a storm come up so fast," Viv pushed her damp, golden hair back from her face. She was wearing one of John's long t-shirts and a pair of his baggy shorts.

"Or so violently." Lin shook her head.

After docking the boat and saying goodbye to Jeff and John, the cousins walked to Lin's house where Queenie and Nicky lounged on the sofas fast asleep. When the girls entered the living room, the two creatures blinked and stretched before jumping down to greet their owners.

"Nice," said Viv. "What if we were robbers? You two need to take house security more seriously."

Lin changed into dry clothes and then she and Viv prepared a pasta bake and a green salad while waiting for Jeff to come by. John had to meet a client and wasn't available for dinner.

"I have a million questions," Viv announced. "But, I'll save them for when Jeff gets here so you don't have to tell the story twice."

Lin was practically dizzy replaying the events from Bakerback Island thinking about the ghost-woman, the storm, and what might have happened to them if they hadn't found shelter in the surfboard shack. Just as she was removing the casserole dish from the oven, they heard Jeff's truck pull up out front.

"Thank heavens, he's here," Viv said. "Now I can start my barrage of questions."

Jeff had changed into jeans and a blue shirt. He carried a plate of chocolate cookies. "I made these yesterday and thought we could have them for dessert."

Lin pressed her head against her boyfriend's chest holding onto the hug just a little longer than she usually did. "I still feel shaken."

They filled their plates and carried the food out to the deck table and settled into their seats.

"So," Jeff swallowed. "Tell us."

Lin rested her fork on her plate and let out a sigh. "There isn't a whole lot to tell. I felt panicky when we couldn't find the kayaks and then the lightning started hitting so close to us. I didn't know what we should do to stay safe. The idea of just plopping down on the ground and hoping that was enough didn't comfort me. I was sure we were going to be struck by lightning." The anxiety she'd experienced during the storm bubbled up in her chest.

"So then what happened?" Viv's face was serious.

"I was looking around trying to see somewhere we could shelter. It was hard to see anything with the wind and pelting rain. At first, I wasn't sure what I was seeing, but then I saw her." Lin's voice was soft. "I thought I was hallucinating."

Viv's fingers trembled as she brushed her bangs from her eyes. "Did the ghost speak to you?"

Lin shook her head. "No. They never speak. This one didn't either."

Jeff could see Lin's discomfort at recounting the episode and he reached over and took her hand. "She led you to the beach hut?"

Calmed by Jeff's attention, Lin's heart rate slowed down. "The ghost looked me in the eye and then she held her hand out to me. She turned and seemed to float over the sand, heading to the back of the dunes to that grove of trees. When she saw

62

that we were approaching, she disappeared."

"What did she look like?" Jeff moved his thumb slowly over the soft skin of Lin's hand.

Looking off to the woods beyond the deck, Lin thought about the ghost-woman. "She had on a long dress, dark blue, almost navy. It had a wide white collar and there was a brooch or a cameo at her neck." Lin's hand moved to touch her shirt just near the hollow of her throat. "The ghost was drenched. Her hair was loose and long and it hung past her shoulders. It was dripping wet. The dress was soaked. It looked like she'd fallen into a lake."

"She led you to the shack? That's how you found it?" Viv's blue eyes made eye contact with Lin.

"That's how I found it. I would never have seen it on my own." Lin wished there had been time to thank the woman before she'd disappeared.

"Do you have any idea who she is?" Jeff asked.

"None whatsoever." Lin bit her lower lip. "I have so many questions swirling around in my head. Why did she help us? What does she want? Who is she? Why is she always soaking wet when I see her?"

Jeff's forehead was lined with worry. "Do you think she has something to do with what's been going on at the lighthouse?"

Lin blinked. "I don't think she has anything to do with the trouble. I don't think there's anything malevolent about her."

"Oh, no. I didn't mean that." Jeff shook his head. "I mean do you think she could be linked to the lighthouse ghost since they both showed up around the same time?"

Lin twirled a strand of her hair with her finger, thinking. "It's a definite possibility."

Viv sat up straight. "Maybe she's come to protect you from whatever bad thing is responsible for the trouble at the lighthouse."

"Maybe." Lin lifted her fork and ate a few bites of pasta. "She definitely wants something, though. That first night she showed up...." Lin gestured to the spot on the patio where the ghost-woman first appeared. "There was a terrible wailing when she was standing there. I wasn't sure if it was the wind or if the ghost was crying out, but now when I think back, I feel like she was making the noise. It happened so fast and I was so surprised to see her. I felt terrible sadness coming from her ... almost paralyzing grief and loss."

Jeff asked, "What did you tell me you felt from the lighthouse ghost?"

Lin sucked in a long, slow breath and realized what Jeff was getting at. "The same thing. Sadness and loss. The ghost-woman *must* be connected to the lighthouse ghost. Benjamin Day. I bet the lighthouse ghost is Benjamin Day."

"We need to find out more about the two ghosts." Viv added more salad to her plate. "What

64

was their relationship? Were they brother and sister, husband and wife? Something else?"

"Right," Lin said. "If we can discover what their relationship was, then maybe we'll be able to figure out why the two of them have shown themselves to me. I need to talk to Anton again and I think I'll make a trip to the historical museum to talk to the librarian and do some reading."

After finishing dinner and munching on the cookies while sipping from mugs of tea, the conversation continued about the two ghosts and what the motivation could be for their sudden arrivals. Lin glanced around the darkening yard. "I was thinking of doing an errand with both of you."

Viv groaned, expecting the worst.

"Tonight?" One of Jeff's eyebrows raised. "What do you want to do?"

"I'd like to go visit the lighthouse."

Viv looked at her cousin like the young woman was mad. "Now? The three of us? In the dark?"

"It's quiet there now. No one is working, the crew has gone home. It's the perfect time to investigate."

Viv scowled. "What is there to investigate? You've been there twice. Why do you want to go out there now, at night? What would we be trying to accomplish?"

"Well, because there are two ghosts now, I'd like to go to the lighthouse and see if either one, or maybe both, show up. 'Investigate' is the wrong word, what I mean is more like, stand around and sense things. Maybe we can pick up something about the ghosts' relationship. Now that they've both been seen, maybe they're ready to work with me." Lin ran her finger over her horseshoe necklace.

"But, what if one is good and one is bad?" Viv offered. "We could end up in the middle of a battle."

"I don't get that feeling. I think we'll be okay." Lin reassured her cousin. "I'd just like to drive over and stand there for a few minutes. We can stay near the truck. We don't need to venture around the property if we feel uncomfortable."

"I'm uncomfortable already." Viv shared a look with Jeff. "What do you think? Do you think it's safe?"

Jeff answered slowly. "I think we should go ahead with the visit. Like Lin said, we don't need to wander around. If anything seems wrong, we can jump in the truck and take off."

"If either one of you doesn't want to go out there, it's okay. I understand. I can take Nicky with me."

Nicky lifted his head at the mention of his name, wagged his tiny tail, and woofed.

"See." Lin smiled. "I have a co-detective."

"There's no way you're going out there alone. Co-detective, or not." Jeff stood up to clear the table. "Why don't we get going."

"And get it over with," Viv muttered.

"You don't have to go." Lin touched her cousin's shoulder. "Really, head home. It's been a long day. Jeff will be with me."

Viv narrowed her eyes. "And let you two have all the fun? Nuh-uh." As she carried her dishes into the house, she glanced back to Lin. "Bring the co-detective with us."

Lin smiled at her cousin, and even though she was glad that Viv would be coming to the lighthouse, she couldn't shake off the feeling that bringing Jeff and Viv along might be a mistake.

CHAPTER 9

The glow from the lighthouse's beam lit up the area at the base of the light, but the drive up the hill had been dark and made darker by the cloud cover hiding the moon and stars. Lin carefully maneuvered the truck into the small gravel parking lot and she and her companions emerged from the vehicle.

Viv wrapped her arms around herself. "I've never been out here at night. It's pretty, isn't it?"

The crash of the waves hitting the rocks below the bluff filled the air and a cool breeze blew in from over the ocean. Nicky lifted his head and sniffed the air before lowering his snoot to the ground and hurrying about taking in the evening scents.

"Stay close, Nick." Lin removed a light jacket from the truck and shrugged into it. "It *is* pretty. The lighthouse looks especially grand in the darkness."

The trio walked a few steps towards the light

when Viv stopped short. "Let's not go any further. I think we should stay close to the truck."

Jeff held Lin's hand and asked her, "Do you want to stand off by yourself so we don't distract you from picking up on anything?"

"Maybe I should." Lin squeezed Jeff's hand. "I'll go sit on the fence railing and try to relax." A low, wide fence rail made of old rail road ties ran around part of the parking area.

"Don't go any further away from us than that," Viv warned. Running her hands over her arms to ward off the chill, she glanced around the property as if she was expecting to see a monster or a ghoul heading for them. "If you don't mind, I'm going to go sit in the van," she told Jeff. "Today's excitement has tired me out. I might doze off. Just yell if you need me."

Jeff nodded and headed off to walk the perimeter of the parking lot.

Lin sat on the low fence facing the ocean and tried to chase the thoughts from her mind by relaxing her muscles, taking in long, slow breaths, and focusing on the sounds of the waves, the wind rustling some leaves, and the chill of the sea air against her skin. When a thought or a question or a sense of unease formed, she acknowledged it and tried to brush it aside.

The memory of the afternoon's wild storm on Bakerback Island flooded Lin's body and, try as she might to push away the panicky sensations she'd experienced, they wouldn't budge. Snippets of the powerful thunderstorm's sights and sounds pummeled her. Feeling like she was back on the beach in the pelting rain, Lin's heart rate increased and sweat dribbled down her back even though she was shivering. In her mind, she saw the ghost-woman reaching out to her through the storm, but this time, Lin wasn't on Bakerback Island. She stood on the deck of a boat tossing on the dark, wild waves in the middle of Nantucket Sound, the wind howling like a banshee.

Lin gasped when, in her vision, she spotted the ghost-woman bob up on a giant wave and then sink back under the water. Popping up one last time, the woman flailed her arms trying to keep her head above the sea, but was unable to battle the mighty swells. Her eyes held Lin's for one long moment before she was pulled under the water for good.

Sucking in a loud breath of air, Lin snapped out of the vision and reached her hands to grip the rail in order to keep herself from tumbling backward. For a second, she forgot where she was and her head moved from side to side trying to recall her surroundings. Rubbing the back of her neck, she stood up shakily and stretched. "Jeff?"

Lin looked to the car parked under a streetlamp and got a glimpse of Viv sitting in the front passenger seat fast asleep, her head pressed against the headrest, her mouth hanging open. Smiling, Lin thought how she would have liked nothing more than to go over to the car and join her cousin.

As she rubbed at her eyes and then scanned the darkness trying to locate Jeff or Nicky, the huge lens at the top of the lighthouse, seemed to spark, sputter, cough, and die. The light was gone.

Panic surged in Lin's chest and she glanced around wondering what to do and who to call. Ships and sailors depended on the light and now it was gone. When the lighthouse failed, did an alarm go off? Was an automatic message sent to the Coast Guard? Did anyone know it had stopped shining?

Lin stumbled forward in the pitch blackness wanting to get closer to the lighthouse to see if she could detect anything that might have caused the light to go out. She took a few steps and her feet suddenly felt like they'd turned to ice. The freezing sensation jolted up her legs into the core of her body and she turned from side to side looking for the spirit that she knew had to be causing her discomfort.

High up on the metal platform that encircled the upper portion of the light-tower, the ghost stood, his body shimmering so brilliantly it was as if the spirit had captured the powerful glow of the light and swallowed it. Lin had to blink and look away for a moment. Shielding her eyes with her hand, she noticed the man was dressed in mid-nineteenth century clothes and wore a heavy black woolen coat. Sandy-colored hair peeked out from under his captain's cap and a close-cut beard covered his cheeks and chin. Lin felt like she was looking up a mountainside at the man who gazed down at her, his facial expression blank, but his eyes heavy with sadness.

Lin whispered, "Benjamin?"

The ghost raised his arm and pointed at the keeper's cottage causing a panicky shudder to run down Lin's back. Before she could turn and look in that direction, the spirit's atoms flashed and disappeared like someone had flicked off a spotlight, and immediately, the light-tower's lens began to work again.

"Jeff?" Lin called out and when her boyfriend didn't answer, she hurried down the dark hill to the keeper's cottage. When she heard Nicky's urgent barking, she broke into a run. Heart pounding, she dashed around the side of the small house following the dog's bark and then stopped short, her throat constricting with fear.

Jeff lay on his side with Nicky standing over him. Lin rushed to her boyfriend, knelt down, and gently placed her hand against his cheek. She whispered his name and he stirred letting out a soft groan. A dribble of blood ran over his forehead.

Lin rubbed his face. "Jeff." Fear made her voice

shake. The darkness made it difficult to see the man's injuries. "What happened? Jeff?"

Jeff's eyes fluttered open and he rolled onto his back, muttering. "Lin." He raised his hand to the top of his head and when he brought it down, his palm had a smear of blood on it. "Somebody hit me over the head."

"Hit you? Did you see him?"

Jeff pushed himself up to sitting position. "Whoever it was, he gave me a good smack." He held out his arm. "Help me up."

Nicky gave the man a lick across the cheek.

"Should you get up right away? Maybe you should sit for a minute."

"I've been sitting."

There was no stopping Jeff so Lin slid her hand under his arm and helped him to his feet. "Are you dizzy?" She gripped his arm to steady him.

"I'm okay. Except for a heck of a headache."

"You should get checked." She helped Jeff walk up the hill with the dog following behind.

"It's no big deal. I didn't pass out, but it was such a good smack, I felt like I needed to stay on the ground for a while."

"Do you remember what happened?"

"I decided to walk around. I thought I heard something down by the keeper's house so I headed down the hill to see what it was. When I went around the corner, I got hit. I didn't hear anyone behind me." Jeff rubbed his jaw. "The smack on my head was so hard, it felt like my teeth were going to fall out of my jaw."

Lin held tight to Jeff's arm and when they were almost to the parking lot, a shock of fear ran through her. "Viv! Is Viv okay?" Their pace quickened and when they approached the truck, Lin could see her cousin still sitting in the front seat snoozing. "Thank God," she sighed.

Helping Jeff to the railing so he could sit down, Lin got Viv from the truck, grabbed a t-shirt from the duffel bag of extra clothes she kept in the car, and told her cousin what had happened while she'd been napping. Lin balled up the shirt and held it to the wound on top of Jeff's head. "We need to report this to the police."

"I should have stayed with you." Viv placed her hand on the side of her face. "I shouldn't have napped. If I was with you, the person wouldn't have attacked."

Jeff slowly shook his head. "It was good you weren't with me. You probably would have been hit, too."

Viv shifted her gaze to Lin. "It was a *person* who hit him, wasn't it? It wasn't the ghost, was it?"

"It wasn't the ghost." Lin shook her head vigorously. She reported seeing the spirit at the top of the lighthouse right after the light went out. "The ghost pointed to the keeper's house and then he disappeared." Lin looked up to the light. "Then the light came back on."

"He helped." Viv nodded. "The ghost wanted to help you find Jeff. The ghost isn't the one who's causing the trouble here." Viv glanced nervously over her shoulder and then stared at Jeff. "If it wasn't the ghost, then *who* attacked you?"

Lin let out a sigh. "*That* is a very good question."

CHAPTER 10

"At least now we can eliminate the ghost as a suspect in the sabotage," Lin said. "We need to report the attack to the police. I think an officer will want to come out here to investigate." Just as Lin was about to pull out her phone, a clanging crash came from the direction of the antique barn and she, Viv, and Jeff wheeled towards the sound.

Viv grabbed Lin's arm. "What was that?"

Jeff turned the beam of his flashlight in the direction of the barn, but the light was inadequate because the distance was too great. He took a few steps towards the structure.

"Wait," Viv nearly shouted. "Don't go down there. We should call the police."

Nicky's barking could be heard coming from inside the barn.

"Nick is in there." Lin's heart sank. She called to her dog and took a few steps down the hill as Jeff swung the beam of the flashlight around.

"Call him again," Jeff suggested.

The dog didn't appear when Lin called a second time, but he let out a bark in response. "I don't think the person who hit you is down there," Lin said. "Nicky's bark would sound different. I get the feeling he wants us to come to the barn."

"Let's go then." Jeff started away.

Viv said, "You just got smacked in the head. You shouldn't be traipsing around in the dark."

"I agree," Lin put her arm around her boyfriend. "Why don't you sit in the truck?"

Jeff smiled at the girls. "You two are worrywarts. The bleeding has stopped. It wasn't a big deal. I was in the military, remember? That whack to my head was nothing." Jeff took Lin's hand and she reluctantly headed down to the barn with him.

"Don't leave me here alone in the dark." Viv hooked her arm through her cousin's and pulled her close. "What do you think that noise was?" Viv eyed the barn.

"I don't know, probably just some tools falling over." Lin kept her voice low.

"Let's hold up," Jeff said. The words were barely out of his mouth when Nicky ran from behind the barn, woofed up at Lin, and zipped back to the rear of the building.

Lin and Jeff exchanged a look, and without a word, hurried after the little brown creature. Turning the corner, they saw the back door of the barn standing wide open. Slowing to a walk, the three moved as quietly as they could to the rear entrance of the antique structure and when Lin and Jeff leaned around the doorway, they saw Nicky standing next to a prone figure on the ground.

The flashlight caught the person directly in the face.

"Kurt?" Jeff hurried to the project manager's side and knelt.

With a groan, Kurt pushed himself to sitting position as Nicky nudged him with his nose. "Jeff? What are you doing here?"

"I could ask you the same thing." Jeff flashed the light over the man's body. "What happened? Are you hurt?"

When Lin knelt on the other side of Kurt, surprise washed over his face. "You're here, too? Oh, this is *your* dog. I didn't recognize him." Lin had worked on a project for Kurt and she'd often brought Nicky to the work site.

With wide eyes, Viv stood at the entrance of the barn with her jaw hanging open.

"You remember my cousin, Viv?" Lin asked.

Kurt gave a nod and Viv lifted her hand in a little wave.

"How did this happen?" Lin questioned.

Kurt adjusted his position. "I think I broke my ankle, or at least, I sprained it." Pointing to the metal staging set up in the barn, he told them, "I was in the area so I decided to come by and take a look around. You know, because of the odd happenings. I thought it might be a good idea to check if everything looked like it was okay."

Lin glanced up at the staging wondering what could possess Kurt to climb up there in the dark. "Did you go up there?"

"Stupid. Yes. I was walking around in here and heard a high-pitched noise so I climbed up to check what might be causing it. I was afraid the bolts might not be tight enough. A flock of bats flew out of the eaves right into my face and I stumbled back and fell over the railing. I gripped the metal and slid as I went down." Kurt held out his scraped palms. "It broke my fall, but not quite enough."

"You're lucky you weren't killed," Viv told the man.

"I'd better call an ambulance," Lin said, pulling out her phone. "You should have the ankle x-rayed."

Kurt gave another groan. "Could I just use your cell phone to call my wife? I broke my phone in the fall. She can take me to the hospital. I don't need an ambulance."

"Let's try and get you up." Jeff slipped his hand under Kurt's arm and Lin did the same from the other side. Viv hurried over to help.

"If you can get your arm over our shoulders, we can haul you up the hill." Jeff maneuvered around to get Kurt into position between himself and Lin and they started out of the door. Viv took Jeff's flashlight and pointed it in front of the three people shuffling towards the parking lot. Kurt had to stop several times to rest which slowed the progress up the hill to a crawl. Just as they reached the top, a dark mini-van tore into the space.

"It's my wife."

The young woman, dressed in ripped jeans and a t-shirt, jumped from the vehicle. "My God, Kurt. Are you okay?"

Lin, Viv, and Jeff greeted Kurt's wife. They stepped to the side for a moment while Kurt was being clucked over by his wife and then helped him into the van so he could be transported to the hospital for an x-ray.

"Well, that was unexpected," Viv said as they watched the van pull away.

"Really." Jeff took the flashlight from Viv. "I'm just glad that Kurt wasn't seriously injured when he fell."

Lin had been quiet while helping Kurt up the hill and into the van and when Jeff turned to her, his eyebrows shot up when he noticed the expression on her face. "What?"

Lin sighed. "Kurt was in the barn by himself."

Jeff nodded.

"Yes?" Viv cocked her head wondering what Lin would say next.

Lin made eye contact with Viv and then Jeff. "How did he get here? My truck is the only vehicle in the lot."

Viv suggested, "Maybe he biked?"

Lin glanced over at the bike rack and shook her head.

"Did he walk over?" Viv looked at Jeff. "Does Kurt live close by?"

"It's not far by car." Jeff's voice held a tone of puzzlement. "But he didn't come by car."

Viv came up with another idea. "Did someone drop him off?"

"Why would he get dropped off?" Lin asked. "How did he plan to get home?"

Jeff nervously ran his hand over the top of his head. "Kurt's a good guy. He doesn't have anything to do with the trouble that's been going on here."

Viv's eyes narrowed. "How can you be sure? How well do you know him? Why was he skulking around in the dark by himself, and how on earth did he get here?"

"It does carry a whiff of suspicion, doesn't it?" Lin looked down at the dog sitting at her feet. "What do you think, Nick?"

Nicky stood up, woofed, and trotted away towards the barn ignoring Lin's calls not to stray.

"Do you think he wants us to follow him again?" Viv watched the creature disappear into the barn.

"So it seems," Lin's voice was tinged with a bit of

annoyance. "He usually listens when I call to him so there must be a reason."

When they got to the bottom of the hill for the second time that night, the three entered the barn. "Is there a light switch in here?" Viv stumbled over a tool box that had been left on the floor.

"There isn't any electricity in the barn," Jeff told them. "That's being worked on as part of the renovations. During the day, we run electricity from the lighthouse." The beam of Jeff's flashlight moved over the walls, floor, hayloft, and ceiling before he shined it on the staging that had been set up in the center of the space.

Lin side-stepped, not wanting to go under the metal rails and flooring of the staging.

Viv eyed her cousin. "Are you afraid to walk underneath?"

Lin ran her eyes over the skeleton-like staging and a chill ran over her arms. "Yes," she whispered.

Jeff sidled up to his girlfriend. "Do you sense something is wrong?"

A flash of something or someone moving over the staging pinged in Lin's brain and caused a wave of anxiety to push at her with such force that she thought she might lose her balance. Her heart thudded as her throat constricted and made her voice sound hoarse. "I don't like it. I don't think it's safe." Lin began to back away.

"I need to check it out." Jeff started up the

ladder.

"Don't, Jeff," Lin called. "Don't go up there."

Nicky barked.

"I'll go slow. I'll check the connection points."

Lin, Viv, and Nicky watched from below and just as Jeff was about to step onto the floor of the staging, Lin yelled to him. "Stop!"

Jeff pulled his foot back and leaned down, pointing his flashlight at the underside of the metal slats. After a minute of inspection, he retreated to the ladder and stepped down. Once on the ground, he looked at the cousins solemnly. "Someone loosened the bolts at the floor connections. If anyone stepped on it, the whole thing would have let go."

Viv gasped.

Jeff found a piece of cardboard and a marker and wrote words of warning for the early-morning crew members who might arrive before him. He nailed the sign to the barn door.

Lin reached for Jeff's hand and anger rose in her chest as she realized what might have happened if her boyfriend had stepped onto the staging.

"Did Kurt loosen the flooring? He was up there on the other side of the staging," Viv asked. "Is he the one who hit you on the head?"

Jeff looked at Lin with a worried expression. "Do you have any sense of who's responsible for loosening the bolts?"

Lin's mind was blank. She shook her head. "I don't, no."

But I will.

CHAPTER 11

Lin and Leonard walked around the lighthouse taking notes and making sketches for the landscaping Kurt wanted done. Despite a sprained ankle and a boot on his foot, Kurt was on-site managing the project and he and Jeff were deep in conversation down by the barn. The night before, a couple of officers came to the lighthouse after Jeff called to report being hit on the head. Lin and Jeff showed the police officers the loosened bolts on the staging and discussed their concerns that the metal connections had been tampered with, but the police didn't seem particularly convinced and offered the suggestion that the bolts had only come loose from use.

"I wasn't pleased with the response the police gave us," Lin told Leonard while making a sketch of the area surrounding the lighthouse. "They think we're alarmists. They told us some kids were probably drinking near the keeper's house and must have panicked when Jeff approached." Lin's jaw was tight. "Jeff didn't see or hear any kids. There wasn't any evidence of beer or wine bottles there either."

Leonard wrote a list of the plants needed for the job in a small notebook. "I suppose it's possible that kids were down there."

Lin didn't say anything.

"Well, isn't it?"

"It's possible, yes, but not in this case." Lin walked around to the back of the lighthouse.

"Do you think all of you were on edge and worked up because of what happened on Bakerback Island yesterday?" Leonard eyed his partner for her reaction.

"Jeff's bloody head wasn't because of us being on edge." Lin made an adjustment to her drawing and tilted the sketch pad so Leonard could see. "What do you think of putting in some tall grasses on this spot?"

Leonard nodded. "It's in keeping with the wild dune grasses. Good idea."

"Let's go to the keeper's house next." Lin led the way down the path and kept her voice low. "I'll show you where I found Jeff last night."

Nicky was busily sniffing along the side of the cottage when Lin and Leonard approached.

"That's where he was." Lin pointed. "Right there on the ground next to the house."

Leonard moved past the spot and walked the

length of the house to the corner of the structure, every so often kicking at the ground with the toe of his boot, and then he turned and came back to Lin. "The ground is hard here. No footprints visible and even if there were, it would be mighty hard to say they belonged to the person who bopped Jeff on the head. Everyone working here has work boots on and has been walking back and forth around the buildings for days."

Lin looked crestfallen.

"Don't get all fussy, Coffin. The investigation is young." Leonard bent to pat the wiggling dog bouncing around his feet.

A voice behind them caused Lin to turn.

"Jeff told me what happened last night," Kurt said. "Is this where you found him?"

Lin nodded and asked about Kurt's ankle. She couldn't help the feelings of suspicion she held towards him.

Kurt shook his head. "You know, we just came off that job at the mansion I was sorry I took," he said, referring to the mansion in town that his crew renovated and Lin landscaped. A skeleton had been found buried in one of the walls. "Now I'm beginning to worry that taking on this project was a mistake, too. I hope there isn't another murder victim buried around here."

Lin nearly choked at Kurt's comment.

"You have some sketches?" Kurt took a step

closer.

Lin composed her herself and turned the notebook so the man could see. "We've just gone over what we think we should do near the lighthouse."

Lin and Leonard took turns discussing the landscaping design and the various plantings they thought would be appropriate and Kurt agreed. "It's just what I was envisioning. It will look great."

A tall, slender man who looked like he was wired too tightly darted up to Kurt. The man had short, black hair cut close to his head like a military officer. His facial features were long and sharp and his movements were quick and rigid as if the man's body produced more energy than his nerves and muscles knew what to do with. "Kurt, I've been looking for you." The man ignored Lin and Leonard until Kurt made introductions.

Kurt gestured to the landscapers. "This is Lin Coffin and Leonard Reed. They own the landscaping company that's been hired to do the design around the buildings."

The man barely acknowledged them.

Kurt said, "This is Jason Grande, the architect hired by the trustees for the project."

Grande unrolled a long sheet of paper and pointed. "The workers in the barn aren't following the plans. This is a crucial part of the design." The architect rattled on about the workers' transgressions and Kurt listened politely.

"Why don't you head over to the barn," Kurt said to Grande. "I'll meet you there in a minute."

Grande frowned, displeased that he had to wait for Kurt to address the issue, but he whirled and practically jogged away.

Kurt rolled his eyes and exchanged a look with Lin and Leonard. "That guy is really strange. He's like a pent-up tiger ... about as pleasant, too. He's on-site nearly every day spreading his charm." Kurt shook his head and returned his attention to the landscaping ideas. "So, what do you have planned for the keeper's house?"

"We're going to walk around the cottage now and come up with a landscaping plan for the keeper's house." Lin was dying to ask Kurt how he got to the lighthouse last night, but she held back knowing the question would sound accusatory and Kurt didn't seem to be in the mood for chit-chat. She and Kurt didn't know each other well and Lin didn't want to imperil the new friendship and working relationship that was developing so she decided to wait before asking him anything about the previous evening.

Kurt started away. "Sounds good. It's a great start. Give a yell if you want me. Off I go to talk to Mr. Strange."

"Is Kurt the one who bopped Jeff in the head?" Leonard watched the man limp away.

"Don't talk so loud." Lin elbowed her partner. "I really hope not. I like Kurt."

The buzz and thump of electrical saws and compression guns filled the air as Lin and Leonard walked the space around the old house. A truck rumbled up to the lighthouse and two men removed two-by-fours from the vehicle's bed.

Leonard returned the workmen's wave.

"You know these guys?" Lin asked.

"I know those two. I haven't seen the others yet."

"There are four more besides Jeff and Kurt. Keep your eyes open. Maybe you'll know them." Lin took a quick glance over her shoulder at the men. "What do you know about those two?"

"The bald one is okay, sometimes arrogant, but gets along with people. The other guy is a bit of a troublemaker. I've heard he works hard when he's on a job. It's when he's not at work the trouble starts. The guy likes his booze ... it gets him into messes."

"Like what?"

"Dumb stuff. You know, fights, driving drunk, some petty shoplifting. He came from a lousy family."

"Would either one of those guys be likely to cause trouble here?"

Before Leonard could answer, a man came up behind them and clapped Leonard on the back.

"Leonard. I heard you were working with a girl." The guy eyed Lin with a creepy smile and chuckled. "I didn't believe it though. It's true, huh? A girl?"

Leonard stared at the man. "Why didn't you believe it? You know I only work with the best."

Lin had subconsciously straightened to her full height, placed a hand on her hip, and turned to face the worker, her eyes throwing daggers at him. When the guy saw the look on Lin's face, he stepped back. "I better get back to work or Kurt will dock my pay. I'll catch up with you later."

"Who was that?" Lin spit the question out as she watched the skinny, red-headed man scurry back to the barn.

"Ned Corey. He worked a few jobs with me a couple of years ago. He thinks he's a good worker. He's not."

"I don't like him." Lin stared after the man.

"Not much to like." Leonard made some landscaping suggestions and Lin drew the ideas on her sketch pad while they discussed the plants, shrubs, and flowers that would be included.

"We'll show it to Kurt and see if he approves." Glancing around the property, Lin put her pencil into her back pocket. She knew that the ghosts would most likely stay out of sight while the workers were on the premises. Even though she was the only one who could see spirits, the ghosts she'd met recently didn't seem to want to materialize when there were other people around. "What do you think is going on around here? Do you think one of these workers is causing the trouble?"

"Maybe."

Lin gave Leonard a little grin. "That isn't much of an answer."

"Like we talked about before, what's the motivation? Why would one of these guys tamper with bolts and equipment? It might make sense if the person was out to get someone in particular, but these things that have happened don't seem to be aimed at one guy."

"Huh," Lin said.

"I've always said you were eloquent, Coffin."

"I'm thinking." Lin frowned. "If there isn't one target, then the person must be aiming to stop the project completely." She tilted her head in thought. "Why, though? Why would anyone want to keep this project from being finished?"

"You're the investigator." Leonard ran his hand over his full head of hair. "Why's it been so hot this summer? I need my water bottle."

They started up the path to the parking lot. "In a few weeks it will be fall and then we'll be complaining because it's cold."

A brown blur rushed past, stopped, and barked three times.

"What is it, Nick?" Lin asked her little creature.

The dog flew back to the keeper's house and disappeared around the corner. Lin and Leonard exchanged a look and hurried after the dog. Nicky sniffed along the stone foundation of the cottage like a wild animal gone mad until he found what he wanted. He woofed again and, for a second, Lin and her partner stood watching his antics.

"He found something." Leonard stepped forward and leaned down near the spot where the dog had shown such interest. "Lin." He gestured for the young woman to come close.

Lin knelt next to the spot where Leonard stood. She peered at the ground, but didn't see anything. "What is it?"

"There." Leonard used the toe of his boot to push the weeds aside and Lin reached out and lifted something from the ground. She stood and opened her palm just as an icy cold breeze swirled around her. When she looked up to the lighthouse, the shimmering ghost of Benjamin Day nodded to her and then his atoms sparkled and flashed, and in a second, he was gone.

Leonard squinted at the thing in Lin's hand.

"What is it?" she asked, holding out a small brass cap about three-inches long by two-inches wide, the top of it formed into the shape of a snake's head. "It's a cobra head?"

"It looks like the decorative top of a cane." Leonard made eye contact with Lin. "Seems like your hound just discovered what hit Jeff on the head last night."

A shudder ran down Lin's spine.

CHAPTER 12

Lin searched the shelves of the historical museum's reference section looking for books or papers on the island's lighthouses. One of the administrators came around the corner with several books in her arms and when she saw Lin she stopped. "Can I help you find anything?"

Lin gave the older woman a smile. "I'm working on a new landscaping design out at the East End Lighthouse and I was trying to find some information about the keepers."

The woman crooked her finger for Lin to follow. "What interesting work. You own a landscaping service?"

"Yes, with Leonard Reed. We've been hired to do some designs that present a natural landscape around the lighthouse property, nothing fancy or fussy that would be hard to keep up." Lin chuckled softly. "Sometimes it's the simpler plans that are the most difficult to do well."

The woman nodded. "I understand. I'm a

quilter and I've found that to be true. A simple design can make a huge impact, but it has to be done right." Stepping up to a large file cabinet, she pulled out one of the drawers. "Here are some articles and stories about some of the keepers. Do you know the years you're most interested in or is it the entire history?"

"I heard there was a keeper named Benjamin Day. I'd thought I'd start with him."

The administrator took a folder from the drawer and opened it to a typed page listing the names of the keepers of East End Light. "Here's a timeline. Benjamin Day, here we are." She placed her index finger next to an entry. "Mid-eighteen-hundreds." She opened the second drawer of the cabinet and removed another folder, this one twice the size of the first. "You can find some information in here. There isn't a lot of material on any one keeper, but if you sift through the papers and clippings, you might find more than you think will be in there."

Lin thanked the woman and sat down at a long, glossy wood table by the windows. Admiring the trees and flowers in the small yard of the museum, Lin took in a deep breath feeling comfortable in the pleasant coolness of the air-conditioned room and began going through the information. Lin had noticed on the timeline that Benjamin Day had taken the position of keeper in 1856 following the mental decline of Nathaniel Mathers. Benjamin had remained at his post for four years and was followed by Jackson Best, who fell or jumped to his death from the cliffs near the lighthouse.

Lin found a copy of an article with a photo of Benjamin standing next to the base of the light addressing a small gathering of people. The story reported that the keeper was giving a tour of the lighthouse to the group and mentioned it was common practice and part of the expected duties for the keeper to lead tours for interested citizens. In the photo, Benjamin wore the same woolen jacket and captain's cap that he had on whenever he appeared to Lin. He looked proud and happy as he pointed to something high on the light. Lin smiled as she gazed at the man's picture.

When she lifted the next paper from the folder, the words "Jackson Best" caught her eye. The man's obituary told that Best had been born and raised in Boston and moved to Nantucket when he was in his thirties. The article listed the names of family members and reported that Best, one of the wealthiest men in Boston, owned several successful businesses, enjoyed boating and worked on boats most of his adult life, and was offered the position of keeper at East End Light after the passing of Benjamin Day.

A friend was quoted as saying that Mr. Best, married with two young children, was somewhat of a loner so the new job was a good fit for his personality and his inclination for a more private life. Best's wife, however, was not of the same mind and she left her husband to return to Boston with no intention of ever returning to island life. The associate admitted that he believed too much time alone was the cause of his friend's demise and spoke of Mr. Best's tales of seeing ghosts around the island.

Lin's hand flew to her cheek and her jaw dropped from reading the words. *Best had seen ghosts?* The obituary went on to report that Mr. Best had been found dead at the base of the cliffs beyond the lighthouse the day after a mighty storm had hit the island.

Mr. Best must have seen the ghost of Benjamin Day. Why would Benjamin show himself to Best? Did Benjamin have something to do with Best's death? If he did, why would he want to hurt Mr. Best?

Lin rested her head in her hand, her thoughts swirling wildly in her brain.

"Excuse me, I have something else you might want to read," a woman's voice spoke.

Lin jumped.

"Sorry, hon," the museum administrator said. "I thought you heard me coming." She placed a copy of an article on the tabletop near Lin. "Here's a death notice for Benjamin Day's wife. I think you'll find it interesting."

Lin's eyes widened as she thanked the woman and eagerly lifted the news article from the table.

"If I find anything else, I'll bring it over." The administrator walked away.

As Lin scanned the old article listing recent deaths, her heart rate increased. One short listing told that Julia Foster Day, thirty-five years old, wife of Benjamin Day who was the keeper of East End Lighthouse, apparently fell overboard on her way to the mainland and drowned during a storm in Nantucket Sound. *Julia. She must be the ghost-woman I see. If the ghost is Benjamin's wife, then why do they always show up separately?*

When she finished reading the few lines of the death notice, a shaft of icy air engulfed Lin so suddenly that she lost her breath for a moment before collecting herself. She shifted her eyes around the research room, but she couldn't locate a ghost. Slight movement outside the window caught Lin's attention and she turned to see the soaking wet ghost standing in the garden staring back at her.

"Julia," Lin whispered.

Tears poured down Julia's cheeks and she leaned forward, covered her face with her hands and wept. Lin's heart filled with terrible sadness. She got up from her seat and moved closer to the window just as the ghost's form sparked and flared and disappeared. Lin placed her hand against the glass. *Come back.*

"Are you okay, dear?" The administrator stood behind Lin holding a stack of books.

Lin took a deep breath and pushed her long hair over her shoulder before turning away from the window. "I saw several hummingbirds flying near the flowers," she lied. "I've never seen a group of hummingbirds before."

The woman hurried to Lin's side to look out the window. "Where are they? Are they still there?"

"They disappeared," Lin said, taking another glance outside to the garden before taking her seat at the table. "But I'm sure they'll come back."

"I hope so." Disappointment showed on the administrator's face that she'd missed seeing the birds. "Are you finding what you were looking for?"

Lin nodded. "Yes, more than I expected. Thank you for your help."

"Glad to help." The woman placed the books on the table to sort through them. "Funny, two people in as many weeks looking for the same thing."

Lin looked up. "What do you mean?"

"You and another person came in to find the same information."

"On the East End keepers?"

"Uh huh, specifically Benjamin Day." The woman checked the spines of the books. "It must be because of the lighthouse project."

"Someone came in recently looking for

information on Benjamin Day?" Lin wondered who had come in and why. It seemed like quite a coincidence.

"Yes, and information on Jackson Best, as well."

A shiver ran down Lin's back. "Do you remember who it was?"

The administrator blinked at Lin. "A gray-haired man, tall. He looked strong and fit even though he walked with a limp."

"Do you know him?" Lin sat up straight. "Did you recognize him from the island?"

"No, but a lot of people come in, tourists, residents, journalists. I can't keep track of everyone. Not sure if he was from the island or if he was a tourist."

"Did he say why he was interested in those two keepers specifically?"

"No, I didn't ask and he didn't offer." The administrator made two piles of the books she'd been sorting.

"Did he read the same things I've been reading?" Lin asked.

"I think so. I gave the same information to him." The woman gathered up one of the stacks and started away. "Do you think you might know him?"

"I don't think so." Lin shook her head. "I wonder why he wanted the information. Do you remember anything else about him?"

"Well-dressed, a buttoned-down shirt and

slacks. I don't recall much more about him. He requested the material and sat quietly, reading. When he was done, he thanked me, said he hadn't found what he was looking for, and left."

"Did he say what he was hoping to find?"

The administrator thought for a moment. "His requests were fairly vague, as I recall. If he'd been more specific, I might have been better able to help him."

"How old would you say he was?"

"Hmm. Hard to say. Some things about him suggested a younger man, but the limp made me think he was older than he seemed."

Lin narrowed her eyes. "He had a limp?"

"He did." The woman spoke over her shoulder. "He walked with a cane."

Lin's jaw dropped. "He had a cane?"

The woman stopped for a moment and turned back, a look of distaste on her face. "He did. It had a bronze snake head on the top of it. It looked like a cobra." She shuddered. "I don't like snakes," the administrator said as she walked away.

A cobra head? On top of his cane? The cobra head Nicky found by the keeper's house must belong to this man.

Who is he? What is he up to?

CHAPTER 13

The sun was setting behind the trees as Lin and Viv sat on the deck of Viv's antique Cape-style house and scooped portions of the chicken pot pie, salad, and grilled vegetables onto their plates.

Lin had been babbling non-stop about her visit to the historical museum and Viv responded to the story with little gasps, eyebrow raises, and jaw drops.

"That has to be the guy who bonked Jeff on the head." Viv's faced had paled. "Who the heck is he? What's he got to do with the lighthouse?"

"I think Jeff should go to the police with the cobra head and tell them he thinks it belongs to the man who hit him." Lin lifted a forkful of chicken pie to her mouth. "This is delicious," she managed as she chewed. "I just worry that the police will dismiss the idea. That cobra head could have been hidden at the edge of the keeper's house for a while. That man might have been visiting the lighthouse and lost the cap of his cane. The police will say it isn't conclusive evidence that the owner of the cobra head is the person who attacked Jeff."

"What about DNA?" Viv's eyes were wide. "A speck of Jeff's blood is probably on that cobra cap."

Lin considered. "It could be, but would the police go to the trouble and expense to do DNA testing on a minor thing like this? I know it's not minor to us, but no one was murdered or anything. I don't think they'd bother."

"Jeff should report it anyway." Viv set down her wine glass. "So the ghost-woman's name is Julia Day. How terrible she drowned in that storm. I wonder why she was going to the mainland. Her husband stayed behind?"

"I don't know. The listing didn't mention if Benjamin had accompanied his wife on the boat or not."

Viv leaned forward. "What if he *was* on the boat with her? Maybe he pushed her over. Maybe that's why they never appear together when you see them."

Lin's eyes widened and she didn't speak for a few seconds. "Benjamin might have killed her?" Her voice was barely a whisper as she looked down absentmindedly at Nicky and Queenie lounging on the grass near the bottom of the deck steps. "Is that why she is so distraught every time she makes an appearance?" Lin let out a groan. "How terrible."

The two ate in silence for a while until Lin said,

"Every time I see Benjamin, I have an overwhelming feeling of sadness ... loss. If he was responsible for his wife's death, why would he give off those sensations?"

"Regret?" Viv offered.

"I don't think he killed her." Lin made eye contact with her cousin. "I just don't."

"Okay," Viv said, a bit of reluctance tinging her voice. "Let's go on the premise that Benjamin Day is innocent. Why don't the two ghosts ever show up at the same time, in the same place?"

"Maybe they can't find each other?" Lin suggested.

"Why do ghosts hang around anyway?" Viv moaned.

"Well." Many times, Lin had thought about that very question and although she had no evidence that pointed to the reason, she wondered if some ghosts hung around in the earthly world because of unfinished business. "The ghosts I've seen lately all had something they wanted resolved before they moved on. The Wampanoag ghost wanted the basket to be found. Amanda's ghost wanted her body to be found. The ghost from the cemetery wanted his bones returned and laid to rest."

Viv stared at Lin. "So some ghosts want an issue fixed, so they appeal to you for help. What about Sebastian and Emily Coffin? Why don't they cross over? Why do they show up every now and then to help you figure things out?"

Lin smiled. "To help me figure things out."

"But don't they want to go to the other side, have a rest? Why hang around here for hundreds of years? Jeez, I'd want to move on. Hundreds of years in one place? I don't think so."

"It's Nantucket, Viv. You never want to leave here."

Viv batted the air with her hand. "I don't understand these ghosts." The backyard was fully dark now and Viv rose from her seat to light the new torches she'd placed around the deck. In a minute, the flames were dancing and lighting up the space.

"Looks nice," Lin said. "It's cozy."

"I want to get a fire pit." Viv returned to her seat and gestured to the spot in the yard where she hoped to place it. "We could sit around the fire after dinner, toast marshmallows." She looked pointedly at her cousin. "Tell ghost stories."

Lin laughed. "That's a common pastime for us. A fire pit would be great. It might help us unravel some mysteries."

The young women cleared the table, made tea, and Lin carried the strawberry trifle she'd made for dessert to the deck.

"I can't wait to try that," Viv said. "I deliberately left room for dessert. I'm practically salivating."

When portions had been placed on small plates

and they'd worked their way through their pieces, Viv leaned against her seat, contented. "Wonderful. I have to hold myself back from devouring the entire thing." She licked her fork. "I've been wondering. Did you ask Kurt how he got to the lighthouse the other night?"

Lin hadn't brought up the subject because she'd felt sheepish about not talking to Kurt about it. "Not yet."

"Why not?" Viv scowled. "You've been out at the lighthouse with Leonard the past few days."

"I'm afraid to ask. It's accusatory to ask him that question and I'm afraid he'll get angry. I don't think he's responsible for anything bad happening out there."

"You can't *not* ask him. He could be the troublemaker. You don't know him well enough to dismiss any possible involvement on his part."

"But Jeff knows him well."

Viv narrowed her eyes. "I think you're probably more perceptive than Jeff."

"I heard that." Jeff came around the back corner of the house and, after greeting the dog and cat who rushed to meet him, he made his way up to the deck where he sank heavily into a chair.

Viv's cheeks flushed pink and she stammered, "You know what I mean ... I didn't mean you aren't perceptive ... I just meant that Lin...."

Jeff smiled. "I know what you meant. It's fine.

Lin *is* more perceptive than all of us." The good-looking young man chuckled at Viv. "I forgive your rude comment."

While Jeff ate from his plate of warmed-up food, Lin told him what she'd learned at the historical museum that afternoon.

Jeff said, "I may as well report the information about the cobra head to the police. I think they'll file the info, but nothing will come of it."

"It's best to tell them," Viv agreed.

"As far as talking to Kurt goes," Jeff raised his eyes from Lin to Viv. "I haven't had the nerve to ask him how he got to the lighthouse either. I worry about causing a rift between us. I can't believe that Kurt has ever done anything to hurt a single person. It's just not in him. He's normal, nothing is simmering beneath the surface."

"He could be hiding it well." Viv crossed her arms over her chest. "If I ever run into him, I'll ask him."

"Yes, please." Lin smiled and nodded as she scooped some trifle onto Jeff's plate. "Then the burden would be lifted from Jeff and me."

"Cowards," Viv chuckled.

Lin ignored the comment. "We need to try and figure out if Benjamin had anything to do with his wife's death. I don't think he did, but it can't be ruled out ... yet. It's odd that the two ghosts are never together. We need to know why."

Viv added, "We need to find out who struck Jeff on the head. We also need an answer to who that man is who was looking for information on Benjamin Day and Jackson Best at the historical museum. Is he the one who hit Jeff, and if he is, why did he do it?"

Lin rubbed her temple. "My head is starting to pound. How are we ever going to answer these questions? Benjamin, Julia, and Jackson Best lived over a hundred and fifty years ago."

"You've solved mysteries older than that," Viv told her cousin. "No pressure, of course."

Lin groaned. "The ghosts aren't being very helpful this time."

Viv placed a second helping of trifle on Jeff's plate. "Maybe that means one of them is guilty of something."

Letting out a long breath, Lin said, "I need to talk to Libby and Anton. I need their insight on all of this."

"Why not send a message to Sebastian and Emily," Viv suggested with a grin. "They could probably help."

Lin said, "I would, but I don't think the mail is deliverable to them."

Viv took another smaller helping of the trifle for herself. "Use Morse code ... send them a smoke signal or something. They must be lurking around here someplace."

Jeff's phone buzzed with a text and he removed it from his pocket to check the message. Lin watched his facial muscles tense as he read the text and her body flooded with apprehension. Queenie sat at attention, her eyes glued to Jeff. Nicky stood up and whined.

Jeff looked at the girls. "It's Kurt. He wants me to come to his house. He wants to show me something. He said to bring the two of you, if you're available."

Lin and Viv had the same expressions of surprise and concern on their faces.

"Now?" Viv asked with a shaky voice.

Jeff nodded.

"Okay, let's go," Lin told her boyfriend, her heart beating wildly.

Now what?

CHAPTER 14

Lin, Viv, and Jeff rode to Kurt's house in 'Sconset in silence each one thinking about why Kurt had called them to his home. Jeff parked his truck and the three were ushered in before they even pressed the doorbell.

"I've been watching for you." Kurt looked over his shoulder. "My wife is getting the kids ready for bed. I haven't let on to her that anything is wrong." He gestured to a room off of the center hallway and everyone filed into his office. The space had two sofas, a television in the corner, and a large glass table with an office chair pulled up to it that Kurt used as his work space. "Let's sit." Little kids' toys were strewn over the rug.

Kurt shifted around on the sofa and ran his hand nervously over his short hair. Lin and Viv sat side by side on the opposite sofa and Jeff took the chair between the couches. They waited and when Kurt didn't say anymore, Jeff asked, "What's wrong?"

Kurt swallowed hard, stood up, and took a piece

of white paper from his desktop. He walked to Jeff and handed it to him.

Jeff read the words and shifted his gaze to his employer. "Where did you find it?"

Lin could tell by the expression on Jeff's face and the slight change in his voice that something bad was written on the paper.

"It was tacked to the door of the lighthouse. I found it this morning, but didn't know what to do with it." Kurt was still standing up. "At first, I thought it might be kids playing a joke. The incidents at the lighthouse have been reported in the island newspaper. Any joker could type this out and stick it on the door."

"But...?" Jeff asked.

"But as the day went on, I got more and more nervous about it. I worried something might happen and maybe it could have been avoided if I took the message seriously."

Lin cleared her throat. "What does it say?"

"Oh, sorry." Kurt took the paper from Jeff and brought it over to Lin and Viv.

STOP THE PROJECT OR MORE WILL GET HURT

Viv let out a little yip and her hand moved to her throat. Lin handed the paper back to Kurt. The man looked pale and harried.

Kurt said, "If it's for real, doesn't the person know that I'm not the one who can stop the project? The trustees are the ones who hired me for the job. The trustees are the ones in charge."

Lin's forehead creased with worry. "I wonder if the island newspaper could print another story about what's been going on at the lighthouse. They could tell about this threatening note and explain that the trustees would be the ones to stop the renovations."

"I wonder if that would help." Kurt let out a long sigh.

"You didn't call the police about the message?" Jeff asked.

Kurt shook his head. "My wife is already on edge about the accidents at the project. She wants me to pull out of it. I didn't want the police to make her more worried."

"I think you need to report it." Jeff's face was serious. "Just in case."

"I know I should. I will." Kurt sat and looked at Jeff. "I wanted to talk to all of you since the three of you were at the lighthouse the night you got hit in the head." He turned to Lin and Viv. "Did any of you see anything? Hear anything?"

Lin, Jeff, and Viv took turns relaying what had happened during their night visit to the lighthouse. Viv made a face. "I was no help at all. I fell asleep in the truck and missed some of what went on."

"What about you?" Lin addressed Kurt, being sure to keep her voice even. "Did you hear anything besides the bats in the barn? Did anything seem odd in retrospect?"

"I was uneasy, sort of on edge, being there alone in the dark. I think that contributed to my strong reaction when the bats flew out of the eaves and caused me to lose my balance." Kurt shook his head. "As I fell, I thought I was in big trouble. I grabbed at the railings to try and slow my descent. The whole thing probably only took a few seconds, but it seemed like I was falling in slow motion and I was just waiting for the impact." Kurt shuddered recalling his fall from the scaffolding.

"Was the barn the first place you checked out?" Jeff asked.

"I walked around the lighthouse and the keeper's cottage and then I went to the barn. Nobody was around, just me. Well, there was one car parked in the lot when I got there and a guy was taking photos near the edge of the bluff."

Lin perked up. "A guy? What did he look like?"

Kurt's face was blank. "Uh, I didn't get a good look at him. He turned around when he heard me in the parking lot and we just nodded to each other as I passed. That was it. I didn't pay any more attention to him."

Lin asked more questions. "Could you see how he was dressed? Was he old, young? Was he short, tall?"

Kurt leaned forward, placed his elbows on his thighs, and clasped his hands together. "I should have paid attention. I don't know. I don't think it was a teenager. He seemed average height, maybe a bit taller. Nothing about him stood out." He lifted his hands in a helpless gesture. "It was so dark. I couldn't make anything out, just the form of a man."

Lin eyed her boyfriend. "That man taking photographs might have been the person who hit you."

"But there wasn't any car in the lot when we arrived," Viv said.

"He could have driven away and come back on foot," Jeff told them. "He might have wanted to see what Kurt was up to." Jeff asked Kurt the question he and Lin had been guessing about. "What made you go out there that night?"

"I just had the urge to go out to the lighthouse when no one would be around." Kurt looked down at the floor. "The things that have happened were bugging me and I wanted to see if it was all quiet or if people were lurking around there at night. I don't know what I expected to see. I'd started wondering about the guys on the crew. I started wondering if there was someone I couldn't trust. I'm concerned about everyone's safety."

"How did you get there?" Jeff questioned. "We

didn't see your car. Did you ride your bike?"

Lin and Viv knew that Jeff was giving Kurt an out … they hadn't seen a car or a bike or any other means of transportation.

A fleeting something seemed to pass over Kurt's face. "I was out for a run. As soon as I left the house, I decided to run out to the lighthouse."

The response seemed off to Lin and while she was trying to figure out why, Kurt said, "You're both working out there. Do you have any idea or maybe a vague suspicion about who might be behind this?"

Lin and Jeff shook their heads.

"I've only been working there for a couple of days." Lin shrugged a shoulder. "I've barely said a few words to the crew."

"I don't have a guess." Jeff looked to Kurt. "I've been thinking it's very probable that it's someone other than a crew member."

"So the sabotage would have to take place when everyone has gone home," Kurt speculated. "It would have to take place after dark."

"Maybe we should take turns watching the lighthouse," Jeff suggested.

"You'd have to stay awake all night," Lin said. "It isn't realistic to stay awake all night and then have to work the next day."

Kurt had an idea. "The trustees might be willing to pay for a security guard. I could bring it up with them."

"Or what about the Coast Guard?" Viv asked. "The lighthouse itself is under their jurisdiction. The trustees are preservationists funding the renovations, they don't have anything to do with the upkeep of the light itself or it's functioning. The Coast Guard should be alerted to the problems at East End."

Kurt's face brightened. "I'll talk to the trustees about reporting all of this to the Coast Guard. The police may have contacted them already, but I get the feeling they didn't, since the cops think it's all just teenage pranks."

Kurt's wife, Robin, popped her head into the office and her eyes widened with surprise at all the people in the room. "I heard voices. I didn't know you had guests."

Jeff stood up. "Nice to see you."

"Come in, hon," Kurt said. "You know Jeff and Lin. And you met Lin's cousin, Viv, at the gala at the mansion a few weeks ago."

Robin smiled at everyone. "Can I get you something to drink?"

Kurt groaned. "My manners. I didn't offer you anything to drink."

"It's okay," Lin said. "We just had dinner."

Jeff told Robin, "We were in the area and Lin had some questions about the landscaping plan so we dropped by." He didn't want Robin to worry over Kurt if she found out that he was the one who'd summoned Jeff to the house to show him the threatening note and to discuss his concerns about the happenings at the lighthouse.

Robin didn't look convinced and she gave her husband a quick glance.

"We should be heading out anyway." Lin stood and nodded at Kurt. "Thanks for letting us come by."

The three said goodbye and left the house. Once they were in Jeff's truck and had pulled away from the house, Viv asked, "What did you think?"

Jeff made a turn onto the road that would lead them back to Nantucket town. "It's definitely worrying that someone nailed that warning to the lighthouse door. The police need to take this stuff seriously."

Lin looked out the window at the dark landscape. Something had been picking at her since Kurt spoke to them.

"Lin?" Viv asked. "What do you think?"

"What?" Lin turned slightly in the front seat to better see Viv in the second row. "I spaced out. What did you say?"

"What do you think about what we just learned?"

"That guy taking the photos ... I don't know. I'm suspicious. I get the feeling he was at the lighthouse that night for a reason other than photographing the ocean in the darkness."

Viv said, "I agree. I think he was up to

something. I bet he was the one who bopped Jeff on the head."

Jeff kept his eyes on the road as it curved to the right. "I think you're both jumping to conclusions without any evidence."

"We're considering suspects," Viv announced. "He can't be dismissed."

"It hurts me to say this," Lin told her companions. "But maybe Kurt is making up the story about seeing a guy with a camera that night."

"Why do you think that?" Jeff asked.

Lin said, "Something seemed off when we were talking to Kurt. Now I know what it was."

Jeff took a quick look at Lin.

"What is it? What was off?" Viv leaned forward in her seat.

"Kurt said he was out for a run that night and decided to go to the lighthouse."

"So?" Viv waited for more.

"When we found him in the barn, Kurt was wearing jeans." Lin paused. "Who goes out for a run wearing jeans?"

CHAPTER 15

Lin parked the truck in front of Anton's house for the last gardening stop of the day and when she opened the passenger side door, Nicky jumped out and zoomed like a rocket around to the back of the house to find the historian. Lin wished she had half as much energy as the dog. It had been a long day of weeding, mowing, and planting in the hot sun and all she could think about the entire time she worked was what Kurt had told them last night. The warning note tacked to the lighthouse door was bad enough, but feeling distrustful of Kurt made Lin's stomach churn. Why had he told them he'd gone out for a jog? He was wearing jeans. It was clear that he was lying to them and it threw them for a loop.

"There has to be a reason he's not telling us the truth," Lin had said on the drive back to Nantucket town.

"What could that reason be?" Jeff wanted desperately to believe that Kurt was not the cause of the trouble at the lighthouse.

"He should just be upfront with us." Viv steamed. "Maybe there's a reason he was at the lighthouse that doesn't involve the sabotage. If that's the case, then just tell the truth. Leave out some details if he wants to, but don't lie."

Feeling betrayed, none of them knew where to start with possible explanations for why Kurt lied about how he got to East End Lighthouse that night so they rode the rest of the way home in silence.

"What's wrong with you?" Anton stood on his deck with his hands on his hips staring at Lin as she approached the backyard.

"Is it that obvious?" Lin sank onto a deck chair.

"You look like you just lost your best friend." Anton sat opposite the young woman.

Lin let loose with a monologue of information. She told Anton that the ghost-woman was probably Benjamin Day's wife, Julia, who drowned in Nantucket Sound after falling from a boat during a storm, that a mysterious man who walked with a cane visited the historical museum looking for information on Benjamin Day and Jackson Best, that she and Leonard found a cobra head cap for a cane near the keeper's cottage, and that the historical museum librarian said the mysterious man used a cane with a cobra head top.

"Kurt found a note at the lighthouse saying that if the project wasn't halted then there would be consequences." Lin went on to tell Anton about her, Jeff, and Viv's late-night visit to the lighthouse property, Jeff getting bopped in the head, and finding Kurt with a sprained ankle from falling from the scaffolding. "Kurt lied to us about how he got to the lighthouse that night. We don't know what to make of it. He could have typed that note. He could be lying about everything."

Anton leaned against the wooden back of his chair, stunned, and uncharacteristically quiet.

"Say something." Lin didn't like Anton's silence. It made her feel like things were hopeless.

"It's quite a lot to take in." Anton's folded hands rested in his lap. "I'm thinking."

"Where's Libby?" Lin asked. "I haven't seen her lately. It might be helpful to talk to her ... get her input, get her involved in the case."

"Libby's on the mainland. I don't know when she's returning." Anton scratched behind Nicky's ears while he thought things over. "So," the historian began, "there seems to be a connection of some sort between the project at the lighthouse, the ghost of Benjamin Day, the ghost of Julia Day, the mystery man, and possibly, Jackson Best, the keeper who took over after Benjamin's passing."

"Why are you saying that Jackson Best is involved?" Lin tilted her head.

"Because this mystery man was looking for information on Best."

"What's the connection between all of this?" Lin lifted a hand palm side up.

Anton narrowed his eyes. "That's your job. You're the one who figures things out."

Lin held the historian's eyes. "There are too many pieces to this puzzle. I need your help."

Anton took in a breath and sat straight. "Let's start with questions. When I begin new research, I always ask questions ... what do I want answered? What needs to be known? It focuses me. Let's do that. What questions need to be answered?"

"Okay," Lin thought about what she wanted to know. "Why are these two ghosts here? What do they want from me? Why don't they ever show up together?"

"Good questions." Anton nodded. "Benjamin Day and Julia Day, husband and wife in life. What keeps them apart in death?"

"Did they fall out of love?" Lin suggested.

"That would be very sad," Anton said, "But falling out of love is not uncommon. Would that alone be enough to have them show up as ghosts in the same place at the same time, each one obviously asking for your help? I feel that there's something else at play here."

Nicky woofed his approval.

"You're right." A rush of energy flooded Lin's body. "Something is keeping them apart. When they appear, they both fill my heart with sadness.

What's the cause of that sadness? I have to figure it out."

Anton tapped his index fingers together. "Benjamin and Julia lived at the lighthouse for several years. The renovation project must be the impetus for these ghosts' appearances. What is it about the project that brought the ghosts forward and brought the mystery man looking for information?"

Lin nodded slowly. "That's the key, isn't it? This all started with the renovations. Why does someone want to stop the project and what about it brought Benjamin and Julia to me?"

"I will see if I can find anything that might help. I'll do some more research. I'll make some calls."

"There are so many things about this mystery that bother me." Lin placed a hand on her stomach. "So many emotions that I feel deep inside."

"Tap into them," Anton said. "Maybe they'll lead you to the answers."

"I'll see what I can discover when I'm at the lighthouse. I'll talk to the historical museum librarian again. I'll ask around about the mystery man." Lin thanked Anton for his help and then she went to work tending the garden, grateful for the hard physical labor of the job that often helped to lessen the stress and worry that surrounded her when assisting the spirits. Her chat with Anton left her hopeful and determined and she could feel her despair melting away as she pushed and pulled the lawn mower and yanked out weeds from the garden plots.

"Lin," Anton called from the kitchen door. "I just made fresh lemonade. Come in and have a glass when you finish."

Nicky, resting in the shade of a tree, lifted his head towards Anton then stretched and yawned and went back to sleep. Kneeling in the flower bed with sweat beading on her forehead, Lin smiled and nodded to Anton. Her mouth watered at the thought of the cold, tangy lemonade waiting for her inside the house.

After placing some new impatiens around the garden border, she stood and dusted the soil from her knees just as a cold shaft of air surrounded her with such force it made her shake. Nicky jumped up as Lin turned to see the translucent ghost of Julia Day standing a few yards away, dripping wet and shivering. The dog wagged his tail at the spirit.

"Julia." Lin took a step closer. "I want to help, but I don't understand what to do."

Tears streamed down the ghost's face. One hand clutched at her abdomen while her other hand reached out to Lin.

"What do you need?" Lin's voice was gentle. "What do you want me to do?"

The ghost didn't move.

"I know that you fell from a boat and went into

the ocean." Lin wasn't sure how much she should press for answers and she didn't want to specifically mention the woman's death by drowning. "Was it an accident?"

The ghost's face hardened and her eyes pierced Lin's gaze like laser beams just as the air around Lin's body became so cold that taking in breaths was almost painful. The ghost-woman's atoms sparked and flashed like bolts of lightning so bright and intense that Lin had to look away. "Did someone push you over the side of the boat?"

The particles of the woman's form flared bright red and gave off such intense heat that it caused Lin to take several quick steps back.

The ghost's form broke apart and, swirling faster and faster, her atoms glowed and crackled and shot twenty feet into the air where they sparked and vanished.

"I'll take that as a *yes*," Lin whispered staring at the spot high overhead where the ghost was last seen. *Someone deliberately pushed you into the ocean.*

Who was it?

CHAPTER 16

Lin sat at the desk in the spare room finishing up her programming tasks for the Cambridge company she worked for remotely. It was nearly midnight when she closed the files she was working on and leaned back and stretched her arms over her head to get the kinks out of her back. The programming work had to be done at night since her landscaping job kept her busy from early morning to almost 6pm each week day and as much as Lin would have liked to give it up, programming paid well and would offer some financial security when the cold and snowy winter months arrived and her landscaping business crawled to a halt.

Lin smiled at Nicky snoozing soundly on the doggie bed in the corner and she chuckled when his small legs began to twitch and jerk from a dream he was having. "What are you chasing, Nick?" Lost in his deep sleep, the dog didn't respond.

Picking up her mug of tea, Lin drained the last bit of liquid and was about to power down her laptop when a thought popped into her head. Checking the time, she knew she'd regret staying up so late, but went ahead with her idea to do an internet search on Julia Foster Day. Sure that nothing helpful would be online about the woman, Lin's eyes widened at the number of entries that filled the screen. She selected one and began to read.

Born to a wealthy Boston family, Julia Foster was an educated woman who believed in abolition and women's rights. Unlike many women of the time, Julia attended a private academy where she studied Latin, Greek, mathematics, science, and literature. Along with her mother, she joined various groups determined to fight for equal rights and the right of women to vote and she spent time fundraising and lecturing for the causes of social reform. Julia and her mother worked alongside Abby Kelly Foster, Elizabeth Cady Stanton, and Susan B. Anthony, some of the leading social activists of the time.

Fascinated by Julia's activities, Lin read for a full hour about her and her family, amazed by the young woman's determination to make the world better. When Nicky rubbed his nose against her bare leg, Lin jumped. "You scared me, Nick." She reached her hand down to scratch the dog's neck. "I wasn't expecting this about Julia," Lin said out loud. "She was a remarkable woman. Wait until

Viv hears about her. She'll love it."

Lin padded into the kitchen to have some cereal before she hit the sack and she fished a dog treat from the cabinet and gave it to Nicky. The dog took his prize to his blanket in the corner near the door and began to work on the rawhide stick held tightly between his paws.

Standing at the kitchen counter spooning cereal into her mouth, Lin thought over what she'd read about Julia Foster Day and pondered who might have pushed her from the boat to her death. *Was it her husband who'd done it? Is that why Benjamin never appears with Julia? Did the death listing mention where Benjamin was that night? Was he on the boat with his wife?*

Lin decided to return to the historical museum to re-read Julia's death notice. It was too late to call Anton, but in the morning she wanted to tell him what she'd learned about Julia's social activism and share her concerns that Benjamin may not have approved of his wife's activities. She hoped Anton could uncover some material that would shed some light on Benjamin and Julia's relationship.

A scraping sound that came from the front of her house caused Lin to freeze in place. Nicky paused from chewing his bone and released a low, deep growl.

"Shhh, Nick."

Peering from the kitchen into the darkened living room, Lin's heart dropped. She'd forgotten to shut and lock one of the windows in the room. She stood stock still, listening, and when all stayed quiet, she shuffled to the kitchen light switch and flicked it off so that no one would be able see her inside the house through any of the windows.

With her heart pounding wildly and her thoughts whirling, Lin wondered if she'd imagined the sound outside of her front window, but quickly dismissed the idea when she recalled that Nicky had growled. They'd both heard the scraping noise.

Was it a raccoon? The wind? A cat?

Scrape. Scratch.

What is it? Lin looked at the dog who sat alert, staring through the living room to the front door. *Is someone out there?*

Lin moved silently over the wood floor to the counter, grabbed her phone and slipped it into her pocket, and then moved to the small closet where she lifted the fire extinguisher from the hook that held it to the wall. Adjusting the extinguisher in her arms, Lin planned to use the object as a weapon if someone broke into the house. It was better than nothing.

A shadow passed over the front window. Lin's heart stopped for moment. *Was he going to try to jimmy the screen on the window? Was he about to break in?* Trying to slow her breathing, she stood still and quiet so the person outside her house wouldn't hear her and know where she was inside.

Hearing nothing, Lin stepped slowly to the door that led to the deck, placed her hand on the knob, and gently opened it. Nicky copied his owner's quiet movements and walked out to the deck. Lin followed and took in a long breath before moving around to the side of the house so that she could get to the front corner. Hugging the dark shadows, she peeked around to the street and then looked over the hydrangeas trying to see the front door. Movement caught her eye down the street to her left as someone turned the corner onto the side road. Under the lamplight, Lin could see a man hurrying away.

He held a cane.

Lin exchanged a look with the dog, dropped the fire extinguisher to the ground, and then the two of them took off down the road to see where the suspicious person was headed. When they turned the corner, they caught sight of the man running along in the darkness towards a van parked at the side of the street. He must have spotted her.

Lin wished she could stop him, but worried the man might have a weapon and did not want to put herself in danger so she gestured for Nicky to hide with her behind a hedge. Pushing some branches down, she tried to see the license plate number, but it was too dark to make out the letters and numbers. The person jumped into the parked vehicle, slammed the door, and roared away.

Rubbing the bottom of her bare feet, Lin sighed at her inability to discover anything about the person who had been lurking outside of her window. It had been too dark to even see the make and model of the car he was driving. All Lin knew was that it was a nondescript dark van. The only clue she had was that the man had a cane when Lin watched him make his escape. *Was it the mystery man?* Lin's breath caught. The man held a cane, but he was *running.*

As she and the dog walked back to their house, anger flooded Lin's body and she clenched her fists. *What was he doing here? What does he want? How dare he lurk outside my home.*

She picked up the fire extinguisher from the small patch of lawn near the front of the house and went inside. Plopping down on one of the stools next to the kitchen counter, she put her hands on the sides of her head and leaned forward, her mind racing. She glanced at her phone and saw a text from Leonard. *Are you okay?* It had come in just five minutes ago.

Lin wondered at her partner's sixth sense which seemed to alert him whenever she was in a dangerous or worrisome situation. She sent a return message. *Something weird just happened.* Lin added details about the man lurking outside her house.

In fifteen minutes, Leonard, wearing sweat pants and an old t-shirt, was knocking on the front door.

"What the heck was that about?" Leonard's hair was disheveled and sticking up. "I'm going to look around out here."

Lin followed the man as he used his flashlight to check the area close to the windows and the small grassy sections in front of the Cape house.

"Nothing," Leonard grumped. "Who was this creep?"

"I couldn't see his face. He got into a car and drove away, but it was too dark for me to see what kind of car it was."

Worry lines creased Leonard's forehead.

"I did notice one thing though." Lin paused. "The guy walked with a cane, but didn't limp."

Leonard's eyes widened. "He had a cane?"

Lin nodded as she led the way into the house, walked to the kitchen, and put the tea kettle on.

"Was it that guy who visited the historical museum looking for information on those lighthouse keepers?" Leonard leaned against the counter, his arms crossed over his wrinkled t-shirt.

Lin gave a shrug. "I just don't know." Her muscles suddenly felt like rubber from the adrenaline rush that had surged through her, and she went into the living room and sank onto the sofa.

Leonard poured the tea into the mugs and placed one on the coffee table in front of Lin. "I'm calling the police. You need to report this." He made the call and shortly afterward, an officer arrived to take a statement and wander around the property.

"Keep the doors and windows locked," the officer advised. "Probably just a weirdo or a drunk, but if he comes back, don't approach or confront him. Call '911' right away."

"I know what you're thinking," Leonard eyed Lin after the police officer left. "I know it wasn't any help to have a cop come over, but at least now there's an official record of the incident."

"That *wasn't* what I was thinking." Lin sat on the sofa with her mug of tea in her hands. Her face was serious. "What I *was* thinking was ... how did you know something was wrong here?"

Leonard stared at his landscaping partner. "What do you mean?"

Lin knew very well that Leonard understood what she meant so she cocked her head and made a face.

"What?" Leonard tried to play dumb.

"Whenever I'm in trouble, you know. How do you know?"

Leonard sat down in the easy chair across from Lin and ran his hand over his face. "How do I know? I don't know. I just get a feeling." A frown formed on the man's tanned face. "It's not witchcraft or anything."

Lin couldn't help but chuckle. "How can you be sure?"

Nicky jumped up on the man's lap and licked his face. Leonard scratched behind the creature's ears. "I don't know how things work, Coffin. Some things can't be explained. You're my friend. Friends have a connection."

Leonard's words warmed Lin's heart and her eyes misted over. He'd never called her his friend before. "Well," Lin's voice was soft, "that's as good an explanation as any." She smiled at the gruff man sitting across from her. "I'm glad you're here."

"It's a good thing you're glad I'm here because I'm staying over in case that fool comes back." Leonard gently pushed the dog to the side and stood up. "Get me a blanket and a pillow. And then go hit the sack. The sun will be up in a few hours and neither one of us will be happy about it."

As she was leaving the room to get the blanket, Lin turned back with a grin. "Are you sure it isn't witchcraft?"

The big man groaned and settled down on the lumpy sofa with the little brown dog curled up on his chest.

CHAPTER 17

Lin had dropped by the lighthouse project on her way to a client to make some preliminary designs for landscaping the area around the barn. She stood at the back of the structure sketching in her notebook when she felt someone approaching.

A gruff voice spoke. "Where's the man you work with?"

Lin looked up to see Jason Grande, the project architect, striding towards her.

"Leonard is on another job."

Grande said, "I wanted to ask him something."

"You can ask me." Lin nodded.

"I'll wait for ... Leonard," Grande said dismissively. "When will he be here?"

"I don't know when he'll be back. You can ask me the question. I'd be glad to help."

"I'll wait."

Lin lowered her sketchbook to her side and gave Grande a pleasant smile. "Leonard and I are equal partners in the business. Whatever you'd like

136

answered, I'd be happy to help you."

Grande scowled. "I don't think so." The man noticed the sketchbook. "What are you drawing?"

"Some landscape ideas for around the barn." Lin didn't share the pictures. She didn't care for the man's dismissive behavior.

"I'd like to see them." Grande reached for the notebook and Lin instinctively withdrew her hand.

"It's very preliminary work," she told him.

Grande took a step closer, his mouth shaped into a sneering smile. "Afraid I won't like them?"

Nicky growled low in his throat.

Lin stood tall. She didn't care for Grande's superior attitude or challenging manner. "I'm not concerned."

"If you're proud of your work, I would think you'd be more than eager to share the sketches." Grande squared his shoulders and looked directly into Lin's eyes.

"They'll be going to Kurt first." Lin kept her voice even. "That's what we've arranged."

"Why? I am a trained and experienced architect. I can give you valuable feedback on your work."

"No, thank you." Lin held Grande's eyes and didn't flinch.

"Where did you study landscaping?" Grande demanded.

Lin swallowed. "I'm self-taught."

Grande let out a snort. The fur on Nicky's back

went up and he took a step towards the man releasing a threatening growl.

Trying not to show how much the architect was getting to her, Lin kept her voice steady. "You said you have a question you wanted to ask?"

"Not of you." Grande's upper lip curled in distaste as he strode away leaving Lin staring after him.

When Jeff came out of the barn, Lin was still watching Jason Grande zooming up the hill towards the lighthouse. She gave her boyfriend an earful about the odd exchange with the architect. "He was so rude to me. He said he would only speak to Leonard even though I told him we were equal partners. I felt like he was mocking me and my abilities." Lin's cheeks flamed red and her eyes narrowed as a growl of anger escaped from her throat.

"The guy's a jerk," Jeff said. "He annoys everyone. Ignore him if he tries to talk to you again." A smile crept over his lips. "Or give him the same treatment. You're certainly capable."

"I will." Lin threw her shoulders back. "What's so great about him anyway?"

"Well," Jeff said as the two started along the path to the parking lot. "He's actually a big deal. He's won all kinds of national and international prizes for his work. He graduated from the Harvard School of Design with a master's degree when he was only twenty. The trustees were amazed that he bid on the project. They couldn't believe that such a renowned architect would consider doing the lighthouse renovation design."

Lin leveled her eyes at Jeff. "This information about how superior he is isn't exactly encouraging me to sass him the way he just did to me."

Jeff laughed. "If he bugs you again, give him heck." He took Lin's hand. "Look, you're intelligent and skilled. Your reputation as a landscaper has spread all over the island and you've only been working for three months. You're in huge demand with very discerning clients. Look at what you've been able to accomplish in such a short time."

Lin squeezed Jeff's hand. "Thanks." She let out a long breath. "I'm still shaken by his treatment though. It was disturbing to be so dismissed."

The two made arrangements to meet later that night at a club where Viv and John would be playing with their band and Lin and the dog drove off to the next client.

***

With the dog sitting near her on the grass, Lin dug into the ground with the spade to widen the flower bed for her newest customer. Sweat ran down the sides of her face and she wiped at the beads of water with the back of her hand.

The house's rear screened door slapped shut and someone called, "Carolin."

Lin turned around to see Libby Hartnett walking towards her. "Libby."

Nicky jumped up and raced to greet the older woman.

Libby wrapped Lin in a hug. "I got back from the mainland late last night. Anton has kept me up-to-date on what's been going on. Come sit with me on the porch. My friend, Alice, owns the house. She won't mind if we talk for a while."

Lin nodded and smiled. "I think you know everyone on the island."

Libby, a distant cousin of Lin, linked arms with the young woman as they walked to the porch. "If you live as long as I have, you end up knowing most people."

Sitting together on rocking chairs in the shade of the covered porch, Lin talked and talked, reporting all she'd learned and experienced about the lighthouse, the renovation project, the ghosts, and the past keepers.

Libby's blue eyes looked out across the green lawn as she contemplated what Lin had told her. "Something very sad is at play here ... and something very malicious."

Lin waited for more.

"Someone is out for revenge over things that

happened long ago. That someone has misinterpreted events from the past and his anger will only make things worse, not better."

"Do you know who is responsible for the trouble at the light?" Lin leaned forward. "Do you know why Benjamin and Julia never appear together?"

Libby shook her head and took Lin's hand. "I can only feel emotions floating on the air. You must be very careful, Carolin. Jeff, too. Keep your eyes open. Stay strong. Do not take chances." After a few moments, Libby said, "You'll figure it out. Keep your necklace on at all times."

Unconsciously, Lin lifted her hand to her neck and grasped the small antique horseshoe hanging from the white gold chain.

Removing a piece of paper from her shirt pocket, Libby handed it to Lin. "This friend of mine has some knowledge of Julia Foster Day. She is a sociology professor and has studied and written about the movement to abolish slavery and expand civil rights. Get in touch with her. She might be able to help."

Libby's friend came out to the porch and the three women chatted for a bit until Lin excused her herself to return to the yard work.

"Keep in touch, Carolin." Libby hugged Lin and then went back inside the house with her friend.

Picking up the shovel and pushing it into the ground to remove the layer of grass, Lin thought over what Libby had said to her. *You'll figure it out.* Stopping for a few seconds, Lin leaned on the handle of the shovel, worry pulsing through her body. Sometimes people's confidence could be a heavy burden. Lin didn't want to disappoint the ghosts or Libby or anyone else.

I have to find more clues. I have to put this puzzle together.

CHAPTER 18

The sky was streaked with lavenders, pinks, and blues as the sun slipped further behind the trees that grew along the bike path. The path was quieter than usual and Lin and Viv pedaled side-by-side enjoying the cooling breeze as they glided past cottages, brush, trees, and ponds. Lin had spent most of the ride complaining to Viv about Jason Grande and his dismissive treatment of her at the lighthouse earlier in the day.

Anger flared in Viv's chest when she heard about the architect's obnoxious behavior and she let a few curses fly. "Why was he so rude to you?"

Lin explained to Viv that Grande was a world-famous architect and that all of his success must have gone to his head. "Jeff told me that Grande annoys the other workers, too."

"Being annoying to people is different than what he did to you," Viv huffed. "He was disrespectful. You're the only woman working at the project. Maybe he doesn't like women."

"I'm going to try and steer clear of him. I was surprised at how unsettled I felt after our encounter. It really threw me off ... it almost made me feel unsafe."

Viv was still scowling about the man and his behavior. "When we get back to the house, we should look him up on the internet. See what we can find out about him. It might be interesting."

The young women pulled their bikes to the side and set them into the metal bike rack. Viv removed a small cooler and Lin carried a blanket as they walked along a trail through the woods. To the right of the path, a clearing of tall green and soft yellow grasses came into view and they followed the smaller trail down to a crystal-clear lake where they spread the blanket and settled down to enjoy the view. Birds twittered in the trees and darted by overhead. In the middle of the lake, a kayaker moved silently over the smooth surface of the water.

Lin leaned back and smiled. "I needed this."

Viv opened the cooler and removed cut-up veggies, a hummus and onion dip, slices of French bread, and cheese. Lin opened a small bottle of fruit seltzer and the cousins nibbled on the goodies.

"I've been thinking," Viv said. "You might like my idea."

Lin looked up from her snacks. "Uh oh."

"That guy who was lurking outside your house

the other night? You said he was carrying a cane as he scurried away."

Lin nodded.

"It could be the mystery man who stopped in to the historical museum." Viv paused for a second. "It could also have been Kurt since he sprained his ankle. He might be using a cane."

"I didn't consider that." Lin's shoulders drooped. "But the man didn't have a boot on his foot."

Viv tilted her head. "I know you don't want the troublemaker to be Kurt, but.... He wouldn't be dumb enough to wear the boot if he was sneaking around your house. The boot would be too noticeable. Kurt could have wrapped the ankle up with bandage."

"Why would Kurt be at my house though? What would be the motivation? What was his plan?" Lin shuddered thinking about someone breaking into her house late at night.

"That's the key, isn't it? Motivation." Viv went on, "What's the motivation behind the trouble at the lighthouse? Who and why was at your house the other night? Why don't Julia and Benjamin appear together? If we can figure out the answers...." Her voice trailed off.

"There are so many parts to this mystery." Lin picked up a carrot stick. "Is everything tied up together or are we dealing with multiple mysteries?"

"Too many questions." Viv rested back on the blanket and looked up at the darkening sky. "And no answers."

"We've figured out a few things." Lin's voice carried a hopeful tone. "We know who the ghosts are and we know that Julia died in Nantucket Sound. I also think she was deliberately pushed from the boat."

"You also found the cobra head thing that goes on top of a cane." Viv added to the list of positives. "The historical museum woman told you she saw a cobra head on the cane that the mystery man was using."

Smiling, Lin said, "See, we're making progress. Slow progress, but still." The smile fell from Lin's face at the same time she dropped the piece of French bread she'd been eating. "The cobra head."

Viv eyed her. "What about it?"

"It's at my house." Lin's eyes were wide as saucers.

"Yeah?"

"It's *in* my house. It seems someone wants it back."

Viv pushed herself up to sitting position. "That's why someone was skulking around your house the other night."

"I bet the person was about to break in, but saw me or heard me walking around in the house." The words tumbled from Lin's mouth in a torrent. "I bet he knew I had the cobra head at my house. He was going to break in when he thought I was asleep. He was going to search my house for it."

Viv pushed her bangs to the side. "He must know you have a dog though. Why break in when the dog is in the house?"

"I bet he was going to give Nicky some tainted meat. I've read about this before. The robber puts some tranquilizer in the meat and the dog conks out."

"Wouldn't it be smarter to break in when you and Nick are out for the day?"

Lin's cheeks were rosy with excitement. "Maybe he didn't want to take the chance of being seen by coming in the daytime. Parking on the side street would have been suspicious. Nobody parks there, everyone uses their driveways or garages. Late at night, the car wouldn't have been noticed because most people are inside asleep."

"There's just one thing," Viv said.

Lin stared at her cousin.

"How would the mystery man know you had possession of his cobra head?"

Lin's mouth dropped open ... but nothing came out.

***

The cousins returned to Viv's house and heated some soup in a pot on the stove. Nicky and Queenie had hoped that their humans had planned a more interesting dinner, perhaps with some chicken or fish, and when they realized that the meal would only involve tomato soup, the animals left the kitchen for the backyard grass. Viv and John's band wasn't scheduled to play at the club until 10pm that night so there was plenty of time for the cousins to have a leisurely bite to eat.

The whole ride back to the house on the bike trails involved speculation about how the mystery man would know that Lin was in possession of the cobra head. The best the cousins could come up with was that the man must have overheard someone talking about the decorative cane topper. "Maybe he was in the historical museum again and heard the librarian discussing the questions I asked her about the man with the cane. Or," Lin said, "maybe the man was standing around near some police officers who knew about us finding the cobra head. That has to be it. It was just a coincidence that he found out that I have his cane topper."

Viv had shrugged. "It's seems far-fetched, but I suppose stranger coincidences than this one have happened. It could also be Kurt. He might use a cane sometimes. He might have seen you find his cobra head at the project. He knew it would be in your house."

Lin didn't say anything. She was trying to come up with why Viv could be wrong, but she wasn't able to think of a reason.

With soup bowls in hand, Lin and Viv sat down at the kitchen table where Viv had set up her laptop determined to look up information about Jason Grande.

"Maybe we shouldn't bother finding out about him." Lin lifted a soup spoon to her lips. "I'd like to just forget him."

Viv tapped at the keys. "You can't very well forget about him since he's on-site at the lighthouse every work day. You'll run into him. It's better to know who you're dealing with." Viv clicked on an entry and read aloud the list of Grande's many accomplishments.

"Jeff told me most of this stuff," Lin said, with a groan.

"This guy is ridiculous. Does he do anything besides study and work? He graduated high school at fifteen, finished college at seventeen, took a year off, and then went on for a master's degree in architecture graduating at the age of twenty." Viv sat back against her chair. "Sheesh. He's like some genius."

Lin chuckled. "I don't think he's *like* a genius, he *is* a genius."

Viv scowled. "He makes us look like losers."

Lin spooned soup into her mouth. "Looking him

up was supposed to help me deal with his nasty behavior ... not make me feel worse."

"Well, listen to this," Viv said. "Grande has never been married and is described as a loner. He isn't a member of any clubs or affiliations outside of his professional associations. No siblings, parents are dead. Probably has no friends since he's so nasty. It doesn't sound like a life I'd want."

"He must have plenty of money," Lin guessed.

"Who cares about money? He has awards up the wazoo and his bank account must be overflowing, but gee, who does he share it with? Who does he care about besides himself? It seems a very lonely life."

"Maybe that's the reason he has such a foul personality." Lin finished off the soup in her bowl.

"I pity him."

Lin held Viv's eyes. "Wait a minute. You're not supposed to be pitying *him*. You're supposed to be pitying *me* because of how he treated me."

Viv sputtered a few words of explanation before Lin nudged her cousin's arm. "I'm kidding with you. His life sounds horrible. Knowing how alone he probably is will help me brush off any rude thing he says to me."

Carrying the soup bowls to the kitchen sink, Lin added, "Or will it?"

CHAPTER 19

A few seconds after Lin and Viv knocked on the door to the sprawling silver-gray shingled house in Shimmo, the wooden door opened and a short, petite, blonde-haired woman in her sixties welcomed the cousins to her home.

"So nice to meet you." The woman's blue eyes sparkled. "I'm Kara Ulrich."

The woman led the way to the back of the home to a large sunroom overlooking the expansive, deep green lawns ringed with flower beds. Iced tea and sparkling water had been set on the coffee table next to cut-glass goblets and plates of cookies and cut-up vegetables and fruit.

"So, Libby tells me that you have an interest in Julia Foster Day."

Lin explained how her interest came about and that she hoped to learn more about the intelligent young woman who had once made her home on the island.

"Julia was a fascinating woman." Kara beamed.

"I found her when I was doing my doctoral dissertation on the advocacy for social change in the 1800s and comparing that time to the fight for civil rights in the 1950s and 1960s. Julia is lesser known than some of her contemporaries, but she was a committed and vocal proponent for social change."

"We found a little about her education and work as a young woman in Boston." Lin said. "We know that she was born to a wealthy family and that her mother shared Julia's interest in equal rights."

Viv smiled. "Can you tell us more about her life?"

"I'd be glad to." Kara set her glass on the coffee table. "Julia was a bright light working for change. She had an amazing intellect, wrote all of her own speeches, wrote articles for newspapers, traveled around the northeast giving speeches and attending rallies for the causes that were dear to her heart. Her mother believed in the same things that Julia believed in, but I don't think she would have ventured out to protest and rally if not for the influence of her daughter. Although Julia wasn't a lawyer, she worked in a law office counseling the poor and indigent about their rights and advising them about their legal issues. Julia's father was a lawyer and he always spoke with her, even when she was a young girl, about law cases and legal precedent and the two had lively discussions about social issues. Julia credited her parents for her confidence and eagerness to learn and said that her mother and father sought out and respected her opinions and encouraged her in everything she did." Kara smiled. "When Julia was asked by her father why she hadn't expressed interest in working at *his* law firm, she replied that she wanted no favor, but to be hired on her own abilities, knowledge, and promise."

"She sounds like a remarkable woman." Lin asked, "How did Julia end up living on Nantucket?"

"As you can imagine, Julia had many suitors. The family was involved in the social whirl of the city's wealthy citizenry until Julia got older and withdrew somewhat from the scene wishing to distance herself from people she felt did not show enough concern about the poor and disadvantaged. Julia met her husband in Boston at a rally. Benjamin Day was a sailor and he'd traveled quite a bit on trade ships. From the things he'd seen, he was very much against slavery and was concerned about the plight of the poor. He believed in equal rights for women. I imagine that Julia was drawn to the man's kind heart and selfless concern for others."

"Julia followed her husband to Nantucket?" Viv asked.

"Because of an acquaintance, Benjamin was offered the position as keeper of the East End lighthouse. It was something he'd always wanted to do. Julia agreed that he should accept the job as long as he didn't object to her traveling back to Boston and the northeast to carry on her work."

"Did the two have a falling out?" Lin questioned.

Kara's forehead creased as she tilted her head slightly. "Why do you ask that?"

"I just wondered if Julia's traveling back to the mainland and being away from home may have had an impact on her relationship with her husband."

Kara shook her head. "I never found any information to indicate that, in fact, it seems that Benjamin fell into a depression after his wife passed away and his health declined very quickly from being so deeply grief-stricken. I believe that the two were deeply in love at the time of Julia's drowning."

"How old was Julia when she drowned?" Viv asked.

"She was thirty-five. Benjamin died the following year, poor man. They had only been married for five years." Kara had a faraway look on her face.

"How do you know all of this about their lives?" Viv asked. "Did they leave a diary?"

Kara reached for her glass on the table and sipped. "You know, there is some mention of a diary in letters and notes that I found in my research, but to my knowledge, it has never been

154

located. I've been able to piece things together about their lives from correspondence between Julia and Benjamin, between Julia and friends and acquaintances, and letters between other people who reference either Julia or Benjamin in their writing. It's very much like a puzzle. A piece here, a piece there, until you get a tapestry of information. Not complete, by any means, but a fairly good picture of their lives and what was important to them."

"Do you know anything about their lives at the lighthouse?" Lin asked. "Was the experience too isolating for Julia? Was Benjamin happy with the work?"

"Julia loved living at the lighthouse. She loved nature and the isolation gave her time to read and write. From time to time, the couple hosted a small gathering of people who worked for the same causes, sort of a mini-convention, if you will. And from all I've read, Benjamin was in his glory at East End. He loved everything about the sea and he wrote in letters to friends how the duty of being the keeper was an honor and a privilege."

Lin took in a deep breath. "Do you know anything about what happened that night on the boat? Were there any witness accounts?"

"Nothing substantial." Kara shook her head sadly. "One man reported seeing Julia near the stern of the boat looking out at the waves. The man walked around the deck and when the storm started to become severe, he went into the cabin. On his way, he noticed that Julia was gone. He assumed she'd gone inside."

"How did the man know it was Julia standing at the stern?" Viv asked.

"It was a very strange coincidence." Kara clasped her hands together in her lap.

Before Kara could say anything more, a shiver of apprehension rolled down Lin's back at hearing the word "coincidence."

"The man knew Julia while growing up in Boston. In fact, he was a suitor of hers. Well, he wanted to be, but she was not amenable." Kara rested back against the sofa. "The man was quite wealthy. He owned many businesses, was involved in trade. He pursued Julia relentlessly. He even bought a house on Nantucket after Julia and Benjamin moved there. The man had married and had two small children, but he couldn't let go of the fact that Julia rejected him when they were younger."

"He still bothered her after he was married?" Viv was appalled.

"So it seems. Julia didn't want anything to do with him. He came from money and he'd set his sights on her when she was just a teen. He was sure he'd win her over eventually. The man was nothing like the husband she would want … he was aggressive, didn't believe in equal rights, the right of women to vote, he thought slavery was acceptable. He thought Julia's activism was horrible and unseemly behavior for a woman of her background." Kara shook her head. "It seems he was a person who could not accept no for an answer."

"He sounds like a nut." Viv's eyes were wide. "How did his wife react to having a home on Nantucket because her husband was in love with another woman?"

"I've never found any information about the woman, no letters, no correspondence.

Lin's heart was pounding. "So this pursuer of Julia was on the boat with her the night she fell overboard?"

Kara gave a quick nod. "He gave a statement that he was on board that night and reports corroborate his claim."

"He followed her around all the time?" Lin couldn't believe that someone would pursue a woman for years after he'd been rejected.

"Often, it seems. He kept tabs on her."

"He should have been arrested," Viv huffed.

"Different times." Kara sighed. "Julia seemed to handle it well, but what she wrote in letters was probably different from what she actually felt about the man."

"Did he leave Nantucket after Julia died?" Lin

asked.

One of Kara's eyebrows arched. "He did not. As I said, this man was very wealthy. He stayed on the island and some speculate that he used his money to buy himself a position on-island."

"What position?" Lin's throat tightened.

Kara said, "He became the East End lighthouse keeper after Benjamin died."

"What?" Viv nearly jumped from her seat.

Lin could barely get the words out. "The man who pursued Julia was Jackson Best?"

"You're familiar with the man?" Kara asked.

"He was keeper for a few years after Benjamin." Lin's head was spinning. "He was found at the bottom of the cliff."

"There was speculation that after she died, Best regretted his obsession with Julia. His wife took their children and left him to return to Boston. He was alone and reclusive." Kara's eyes widened. "Let me show you something." She stood and retrieved her laptop from a desk in the corner. Tapping at it, she found what she was looking for and adjusted the screen for Viv and Lin to see. "Jackson Best was an amateur artist. He drew from the time he was a little boy. Here are some of his pictures on this historical website."

"Those are pretty good," Viv said as she looked at drawings of seascapes and landscapes.

Kara hit a few keys and another row of pictures

came up on the screen that were darker and more ominous than the previous artwork. "These were done after Julia drowned." The woman made eye contact with Lin and Viv. "It seems that Jackson Best went off the deep end during his time as keeper. He claimed to see ghosts."

Lin couldn't suppress a gasp.

"You can see here and here," Kara pointed. "He drew ghosts in places throughout Nantucket, over and over in these later paintings, ghosts appear. Always women ghosts. It's assumed that Best went mad and ended up hurtling himself off the cliffs to his death."

"What an awful story," Viv rubbed her temple.

"Three very sad ends." Kara nodded. "Julia, Benjamin, and Jackson Best. Lives intertwined, and not with a good outcome."

When the visit was over and the cousins were in Lin's truck heading back to Nantucket town, Lin said to Viv, "Jackson Best killed Julia. I know it as sure as if I was standing there on that boat deck watching him do it." She set her jaw. "One more piece to this puzzle."

CHAPTER 20

Jeff met Lin in the parking lot of the lighthouse and the two walked down to the keeper's cottage. The other workers had gone to two other jobs for the afternoon and Kurt stayed home to rest his ankle so Jeff was the only one on-site for the remainder of the day. He'd recently started work on the interior of the cottage and he thought Lin might like to look around inside so he'd texted her and asked her to come by.

"I'm a little nervous about being in the house." Lin tightened her grip on Jeff's hand.

"I'll be with you the whole time. No one's here except us."

Nicky hurried ahead wagging his tail eager to go into the cottage.

Lin had told Jeff the news she'd learned about Julia and Benjamin and Jackson Best and her suspicion that Jackson was the one who pushed Julia from the boat into Nantucket Sound. "A stalker, huh?" Jeff had said. "I was naïve to think stalking was a modern problem."

Lin still couldn't wrap her head around the idea that Jackson Best was so infatuated with Julia, despite their deep philosophical differences about life and what was important, that he'd followed her to Nantucket even though he was married to another woman and had children with her. The man was seriously disturbed and allowed his obsession to ruin his life.

"He drew ghosts around Nantucket," Lin told Jeff. "The ghost in his pictures was a woman, always the same woman."

Jeff stared at Lin. "You think he saw Julia's ghost? You think Julia haunted him?"

Lin winced at the word "haunted" and Jeff apologized when he saw her reaction and reworded his sentence. "Do you think Julia appeared to Mr. Best after he killed her?"

Lin nodding slowly. "I think she did. Once when I saw her and asked if she'd been pushed over the rail of the boat, her atoms, or whatever makes up the spirit, turned bright red and flared into the air. I think Julia was so enraged about what Jackson had done to her and Benjamin that she couldn't cross over and kept appearing to him until he ended up killing himself." Lin quickly added, "I don't think Julia's intention was for Best to kill himself. I think she only wanted to confront him for what he'd done."

Jeff eyed his girlfriend and asked with a touch of wariness in his voice. "Have you ever seen the ghost of Jackson Best?"

"Never."

"I just wondered. If he *was* around, I might put my money on him being the one who has been trying to sabotage the lighthouse project."

"Why would he want to do that?"

"In some sort of rage, Jackson Best killed the woman he thought he loved. If Julia hadn't married Benjamin, she wouldn't have been on that boat. I bet Best was full of remorse. Then Julia appeared to him and he started to go crazy knowing that he'd lost all chance to ever be with her. He must hate the lighthouse ... it's the symbol of his loss."

Lin was stunned by Jeff's suggestions. It all made perfect sense. The only problem with the theory was that Lin had never once seen the ghost of Jackson. Nervousness flared in her chest ... *what if he keeps himself hidden from me? If his goal is to destroy the project or maybe even the lighthouse, then he doesn't want anything from me. How do I fight a ghost I can't see?*

Lin tried to quell her panic and forced herself to think through the possibility. "I think I'd sense his presence even if he stayed hidden so I don't think he's around." *At least I hope he isn't.*

Jeff opened the door of the keeper's cottage.

"The interior is going to look great when the renovations are complete. The place is actually bigger than it seems from the outside."

Jeff led the way through the rooms and as Lin looked around, she got caught up in admiring the period details of the home and her unease began to ebb away.

"It's really lovely." Lin smiled. "I know it's a huge mess, but I can imagine the cottage as it was in the 1800s. It must have been comfortable and homey." She pointed at the stone fireplace, the wood floors, the good-sized windows allowing sunlight to stream over the walls. "I love it."

"I feel the same way." Jeff indicated the charming characteristics of the place as they made their way through the rooms. "I feel honored to be able to help restore the home."

When they'd finished the tour, Jeff asked if Lin had "felt" anything in any of the rooms.

"I didn't. Maybe I'll wander around for bit while you work and try to sense something."

Nicky woofed from the living room and the young couple returned the front room to find the dog sitting in the rocking chair.

Lin chuckled. "Okay, Nick. I get the message." As Lin approached the chair, the little brown dog jumped down and curled up on a tattered rug in front of the fireplace. Lin brushed some dirt and dust from the seat and eased herself onto the rocker. "I can feel some energy in this room. I'll sit here and see if I can tap into whatever might be floating on the air."

Jeff nodded and headed to the rear of the cottage to continue his work. "Just yell if you need me."

Settled in the rocker with the sun shining on her through the window, Lin glanced out to the yard. There was a lovely view of the lighthouse rising up like a red and white mountain to protect the boats at sea. With her muscles relaxing from the gentle back and forth of the chair's movement and the warmth of the sunlight, Lin's eyelids started to droop. Nicky snored from his position on the rug and in a few minutes, she joined the dog in slumberland.

Lin's lids fluttered open and she saw a sandy-haired man sitting at a desk across the room, his back to her as he hunched over his work writing in a leather notebook. Glancing down at her knees, Lin was surprised, but not alarmed, to see that she was no longer wearing her jeans, but was clothed in a long, pale blue dress of soft cotton. Reaching to her neck, she felt a brooch at her collar.

The light was low and fading as the sun crept below the bare trees and the room began to fill with shadow as a fire burned in the fireplace chasing the chill of the winter evening from the room. Watching the man at the desk scribbling away, a flood of contentment filled her heart.

"Are you sure you don't want me to come with you tomorrow?" The man spoke to her without turning or looking up. "I'm sure that Thomas Monson would watch the lighthouse for me while I was gone."

"No need," a woman replied.

Lin knew that the woman who answered was sitting in the rocker and that what she felt, saw, and heard was *that* woman's experience and not her own.

"I can manage it," the woman told the man who chuckled at her response.

"I have no doubt in my mind that there is nothing you cannot handle, my dear."

The lovely image faded and a different experience took its place.

A heavy hand pounded on the cottage's front door. Boom. Boom. The house practically shook. A woman stood a foot from the door holding the fireplace poker in her hands. "Go away, Jackson." Her voice was firm, but Lin could make out the slight tremor of fear. "Stop coming here. Go home to your wife."

The pounding on the door was so fierce that Lin worried the wood might split in half and allow the unwanted visitor entry to the home.

"I will have *you* for my wife. You, Julia."

"Leave me alone. Leave us alone," Julia shrieked. "Benjamin will be home soon. Go away,

Jackson."

The next image showed Julia slumped to the floor still holding the fireplace poker across her lap. The man must have gone, because all was quiet ... except for the soft weeping of the woman collapsed against the door.

Covered with sweat and her heart in her throat, Lin woke with a start. Nicky whined at his human, his head pressed against her leg.

"I'm okay, Nick." Lin ran her hand over the dog's soft fur as Jeff bolted into the room carrying a hammer like a weapon.

Lin met the handsome carpenter's eyes. "I'm okay."

Jeff knelt by the rocker and took her hand. "You were shouting. I couldn't make out the words. Was it a dream?"

"It was more of a vision." Lin told him what she'd seen and heard. "It was horrible, Jeff. I could feel the fear coursing through Julia's body. Jackson Best sounded out of his mind. Poor Julia."

Jeff gently moved a strand of hair from Lin's eyes. "Best arranged travel on the same boat as Julia when she made the trip to the mainland so that he could confront her again. They must have fought."

"He pushed her overboard." Exhausted by the experience, Lin pressed her head against the chair back and glanced over to the empty corner of the room where Benjamin had sat at the desk in the vision. Something pinged in her head, but it jumped away before she could grasp it.

CHAPTER 21

Lin and Viv strolled into town under the twinkling streetlamps to do some shopping and walk along the docks to admire the huge yachts that showed up every summer. Occasionally they spotted a few celebrities partying on the massive vessels or a well-known politician sitting with friends on the upper deck of a ship sipping a drink. Viv always got a thrill out of seeing one of the rich and famous who came to enjoy the beautiful island and she counted Academy Award winners, reality TV stars, writers, two vice-presidents of the United States, senators, congresspersons, and famous fashion designers among the people she'd caught in her sights.

"Maybe tonight we'll be able to add someone new to your list of sightings," Lin kidded her cousin.

"As long as the person is alive." Viv smiled. "Ghosts don't count, no matter who they used to be, so if you see one, don't bother telling me."

"I've never seen the ghost of a famous person,"

Lin mused. "That would be pretty cool."

Weaving around tourists and townspeople, the two discussed who from the past would be the most exciting person for Lin to see as a ghost.

"Abraham Lincoln," Lin said.

"Well, since I own a bookstore, how about Mark Twain?"

"Hatshepsut."

"Who?" Viv scrunched up her face.

"She was a pharaoh in ancient Egypt."

"A woman was a pharaoh?"

Lin nodded. "It was rare, but, yup, Hatshepsut was a pharaoh."

"Not her. She'd probably scare me," Viv said. "I'd prefer Mary Shelley or Emily Dickinson. Oh, what about Agatha Christie? She'd make an interesting ghost."

The two went on with their game until Lin's phone buzzed with a text from Anton who asked if the cousins could meet him at one of the restaurants down by the docks. He was with someone he thought they should meet.

The girls exchanged looks and then hurried away to find Anton and his mystery person. Entering the busy establishment, they finally spotted the historian waving them over to a long table positioned by the windows. Anton had pulled up to two empty chairs for the young women.

"Lin, Viv, this is Abigail Getty and her daughter,

Windsor Smith. I've known Abigail for years, I
won't say for how many years. She is a history
professor at Wellesley. Windsor is an architect.
She's here on-island to do some work for a new
client."

As the members of the group greeted one
another, Lin made eye contact with Windsor
thinking that meeting the young woman must be
the reason Anton had called them to the restaurant.

Anton spoke. "We've been talking about what's
been going on around here lately. I brought up the
strange goings-on at the lighthouse." The historian
paused. "Windsor happens to know the architect
who is working on the project."

Lin and Viv turned to the woman.

"I don't know him well." Windsor sniffed and
pushed her black hair over her shoulder. "I don't
care to know him well. I was extremely surprised to
hear he was on Nantucket."

"Have you worked with him?" Lin asked.

"I went to school with him and also had the
misfortune to work with him on a project in Europe
not long after graduation. Jason whipped through
the program in record time. I wasn't a star or
anything, but I did well."

"You don't have a high opinion of him?" Viv
asked.

"I have a high opinion of his work." Windsor's
face clouded. "I don't have a high opinion of him as

a person. No one wanted to work with him. If Jason was in your working group, he would take over the project. He wouldn't listen to anything the other students suggested. He was verbally abusive. Jason was belittling and demeaning, especially to any women in the group. He'd say nasty things to the women like, why don't you go home and bake some cookies, you have no business taking a man's spot at this school." Windsor rolled her eyes. "It was like we were living in a time warp."

Lin asked, "Did you have a run-in with him?"

"Everyone had a run-in with him. Most people just wanted to avoid the man. The program was demanding, very time-consuming. No one needed the extra problem of Jason Grande." Windsor sighed. "There was a competition. I won't go into details, but Jason stole my ideas and passed them off as his own. He won the competition."

"Did you report him?" Viv's face flushed with anger.

"What good would it do? Jason was a star. Who would believe me that *he* took *my* ideas? It would have made me look foolish, like I was acting out my jealousy. No one would believe my claim. Jason was so talented, no one could imagine that he would stoop to taking another student's idea, he didn't need to."

"Why did he do it then?" Viv's cocked her head.

"It was another way to demean us. Jason could

design circles around us, but he enjoyed playing games with his peers, messing with our heads, finding ways to put us down. He's a sociopath."

"I'm not surprised at his behavior, but I am surprised at the level of his behavior." Lin rubbed her temple. "Anton told you about his exchange with me? It was so minor in comparison to what you and the other students had to deal with. I've managed to avoid him lately."

"Avoidance is the best thing." Windsor nodded. "I was shocked when Anton told us that Jason was working on the lighthouse. That isn't a project that he would give a second glance. It's not high-profile enough for him. It makes me wonder what he's up to."

"Really?" Lin asked. "The lighthouse is a national treasure. Wouldn't that be prestigious enough for him?"

Windsor laughed. "Are you kidding? Jason only works on the projects that will be noticed across countries. He wouldn't stoop to a project this unimportant in his eyes ... unless there's something in it for him." The woman nodded at Anton. "We've spent an hour trying to figure out what that might be. We've come up empty."

Lin's shoulders drooped. The discussion wouldn't help to figure out who was sabotaging the project or why the two ghosts had appeared to her.

Viv piped up. "It would make no sense to think

that Jason was involved in the accidents at the project. Why would he want the project to stop?"

"Maybe he doesn't want the project to stop," Windsor offered. "Maybe he's playing with the workers the way he played with us when we were in graduate school. Maybe Jason wants to look like the hero here. The project succeeded because he would not relent, he would not be cowed by fear, he will be the savior of the project."

Anton shrugged. "Perhaps the man feels he needs to turn his press around. He is difficult and has a reputation as a monster. He may have caused the issues at the lighthouse to enhance his reputation as one who won't allow problems of any kind to stop what he has promised to do."

Lin let out a long breath. "I don't know. Grande doesn't seem like someone who cares about that sort of thing. He wants acclaim for his work, yes, but I don't think he cares what people think of him personally."

Viv brought up what she and Lin had read online. "He seems to have a very lonely life. He's never married? Has he ever had a girlfriend?"

"Jason has never been married. At school, he made some weird attempts at dating. Women declined his offers. A friend of mine saw him at a bar once. He came in, looked around like he was picking out a ham in a grocery store, approached the woman next to my friend, and proceeded to grope her. When she protested, he tried to strike her. My friend's boyfriend stepped in and removed Jason from the bar. That was Jason's idea of a date." Windsor harrumphed. "No woman in her right mind would take his abuse." She made eye contact with Lin. "Stay far away from Jason Grande. His head is screwed on incorrectly. Keep your eyes open whenever he's around."

Regret that she'd taken the landscaping job at the lighthouse pulsed though Lin's head. She didn't want anything to do with the nasty architect and she didn't care what his motivation was for taking the project. The ghosts were her priority. She needed to help them. *But how? What did they want? Why don't they ever appear together?* Lin's head pounded. She wanted to get outside into the fresh air and clear her head of what she'd just heard.

Standing up, she thanked Windsor for the information and gave Anton a hug. As she reached across the table to shake hands with the young woman and her mother, Windsor shook her head. "For the life of me, I can't figure out why Jason would agree to design a project that was located on an island."

A shiver of unease ran down Lin's back. "Why do you say that?"

"He has some odd aversion to beaches and the seacoast. Jason hates islands. He hates anything that's nautically related."

Lin's stomach clenched.

CHAPTER 22

Nicky led Lin through town and down the brick sidewalks to Viv's bookstore. When they entered, Queenie sat regally waiting for them inside just a few feet from the door with her long gray tail curled around her feet. The dog's stubby tail wagged crazily when he spotted the cat and he dashed to her and gently touched his snoot to her little pink nose before the two took off to the back of the store.

Lin smiled at the two creatures as they disappeared around the end of a long bookshelf on their way to their favorite easy chair. Viv stood behind the check-out counter preparing the cash registers and making sure there were enough tissue paper and paper bags to wrap the customers' purchases in.

"Want any help?" Lin asked.

Viv looked up. "Thanks, no. I'm almost done." After adding more bags to the shelf under the cash register, she came out from behind the counter. "Come to the café with me. We can talk there."

The cousins headed to the rear of the store where they worked together to stock the needed supplies. After Lin and Viv met Anton and his friends at the dockside restaurant the previous evening, they went to Viv's gig at a downtown pub and had barely any chance to talk about what they'd learned from Windsor Smith.

"What do you think about what Windsor told us?" Viv restocked the napkin holder.

Lin slowly shook her head. "I think Jason Grande is weirder than I thought."

"How about that stuff Windsor said about Jason hating anything nautical."

Lin filled the sugar dispensers. "What an odd aversion. What would make him dislike islands? Some strange tic? At that point, I'd had enough of listening to tales of the oddball. Actually, I'd had enough of hearing about the man before Windsor told us that tidbit."

Viv surmised. "Maybe he got pulled under the waves when he was a kid and got traumatized."

"And ever since, he hates water and beaches and nautical things? He must have been truly scarred." Lin shook her head at the absurdity of it all. "I don't care about him. I need to focus on the ghosts."

"Have you seen either one of them recently?" Viv carried a tray of sticky buns to the bakery display case.

"I haven't." Lin sat on one of the counter stools while she unwrapped stacks of take-out cups.

"Maybe the ghosts have gone away." Viv heated water for tea. "Maybe they tired of how slow you were to help them."

"Thanks a lot." Lin gave her cousin the evil eye.

"I'm kidding with you. I'm sure they're not gone. They're lurking in the shadows somewhere around here." Just as Viv chuckled, a tray of washed mugs tipped off the end of the counter and crashed to the floor.

Both girls jumped.

Viv's hand flew to her throat. "Oh, gosh. The ghosts must have heard me." She pointed to the dishes broken on the floor. "They did this, didn't they?"

Lin scurried to the broken mugs with a dustpan and brush and began sweeping up the shards of glass. "It wasn't a ghost. The tray must have been too close to the edge." Despite her words of comfort to her cousin, Lin glanced around looking for a ghost.

When the mess was cleaned away, Viv eyed Lin. "What's the next step? What are you going to do next to figure out what the ghosts want from you?"

"I honestly don't know." Lin sipped from the teacup her cousin had placed in front of her. "You know ... the living room of the keeper's cottage keeps popping into my head. All of a sudden, I picture it in my mind or I remember the feeling I had when I was sitting in the rocking chair. As soon as I came out of the vision I had, I was staring into the corner of the room where I'd seen Benjamin Day writing at his desk. I had an odd sensation run through me like there was something important about that corner, but then the feeling dissolved and I couldn't grasp what it was." Lin held her cousin's eyes. "Now I can't stop thinking about that room, that corner. I feel a pull to go back in there."

Viv stared at Lin for a few moments. "Then, go back."

"It's not that easy," Lin frowned. "There are people working there all day. I don't have anything to do with the interior. I can't just wander in when the carpenters are working, sit down in that rocker, and space out ... and even if I could do that, I don't think I would be able to sense much when the other people are in there."

Viv bit her lip, thinking. "What if you ask Jeff to tell Kurt he'd like to stay late to work at the keeper's house some night and could he have the key to the cottage?"

"I wonder if Kurt would let Jeff have it."

Viv tapped the counter with her index finger. "There's one way to find out."

***

Lin and Jeff walked hand in hand through the pitch darkness of the night down the hill to the keeper's cottage. When Jeff asked if it might be possible to work late one night, Kurt didn't hesitate to give him the key.

After he'd had dinner, Jeff returned to the cottage to work and, as they'd planned, waited for Lin to arrive once darkness fell.

Jeff placed the key in the new lock and pushed the door open. He turned on one of the work lamps that were scattered around the cottage and the room flooded with bright light causing Lin to close her eyes briefly against the glare.

"I'd like to sit or walk around in here." Lin stepped slowly around the sitting room. "Could we move the lamp to the doorway into the next room? I think less light would be helpful."

Jeff carried the work lamp to the threshold between the rooms and set it down. "Better?"

"Much better." Lin gave him a smile.

"I'll go to the back room. I'll be making noise with saws and drills. Will that be okay?"

Lin nodded as she stepped to the fireplace. "Yes, that won't bother me."

"You know where to find me if you need me." Jeff left Lin alone and headed to the rear of the cottage.

Taking in a deep breath, Lin tried to clear her

mind in order to be open to anything she thought the room might tell her. She glanced over to the corner where Benjamin had sat at a desk in her vision. Taking slow steps to the corner, she stood and closed her eyes for a full minute without picking up on anything except the chill of the unheated house. She crossed the space to the antique rocker and sank into it with her hands resting on the old wood of the chair's arms. Her hands could feel the years of grime that had collected over the wood and for a moment, Lin wondered how no one had stolen the rocking chair from the keeper's cottage. Since the lighthouse had become automated and no keeper was needed to live in the small house, most everything had been removed or stolen from the place, but Lin knew that sometimes things got left behind.

She waited for some of those remaining things to float by on the air, and in a few minutes, Lin was asleep in the chair.

***

Nearly an hour later, Jeff gently shook Lin's arm and she woke with a start.

Looking around, disoriented, Lin rubbed her forehead. "I fell asleep."

"I see that." Jeff chuckled. "Did you...?"

"Nothing." Lin sat straighter to stretch her back.

"Last time, I fell into a sleep and I had the vision. Nothing happened this time."

Jeff sat on the floor next to the rocker. "Do you think the ghosts have gone away?"

"I wonder." Lin looked crestfallen. "But, why would they? I haven't helped them yet."

"Do you want to go home?"

"I guess so." Lin stood up reluctantly and as she took Jeff's hand, a whoosh of icy air engulfed her.

"It's freezing in here." Heading for the door, Jeff shuddered.

Lin stopped, let go of his hand, and stared at her boyfriend, dumbfounded that he could feel the cold air surrounding her and then she flashed her gaze about the room trying to locate the ghost. The room was empty.

"Lin?"

Just as she turned her attention back to Jeff, an odd crackling sound filled the air. "Do you hear that?"

"Hear what?" Jeff questioned.

"A buzzing noise. A crackling." Lin moved around trying to determine where the sound was coming from. "You don't hear it?"

"I don't hear anything."

When Lin stepped into the corner where Benjamin had been in her vision, the sound grew so loud that she couldn't hear what Jeff was saying to her. She put her hands over her ears and shook her head. As the buzzing intensified, pain pulsed in her eardrums and the room began to spin so fast that Lin reached out to place her hand on the wall. When her skin touched the old wood, jabs of electricity zapped her fingers and before she could pull away, the crackling noise ceased and her hand felt a surge of warmth.

"Jeff."

He hurried to her side and gently touched Lin's arm.

"I think there's something here." Lin lowered her hand on the wall and the sensation of warmth increased. Continuing to follow the feeling of growing heat, Lin knelt, her hand at the bottom of the old wall. "It's here, right behind this section."

Jeff rushed to the back room to get some tools and then knelt beside Lin to pick away at the spot. Pieces of plaster came loose to reveal a hole in the wall. Jeff shined his flashlight into the spot, reached his hand inside, and when he pulled his hand out, he held a small, dusty leather book. Placing it in Lin's hands, a smile spread over his face and he said, "You just never know what you'll find in old houses."

CHAPTER 23

Lin read aloud from Benjamin Day's old diary to the people who had gathered around her kitchen table. Viv and Anton responded to the late-night call to meet at Lin's house and the two sat with Jeff listening to Lin read parts of the diary.

The leather book contained entries detailing Benjamin and Julia's days at the lighthouse ... their duties, the weather, the beauty of the island, and their joy at living and working in such a beautiful place so close to nature. Lin read that Julia had started a garden ... a ship ignored the lighthouse's warning and ran aground on the rocks ... Benjamin worked to fix up the keeper's cottage to his and his wife's liking. The man wrote movingly of missing his wife when she traveled to the mainland to take part in rallies and to give speeches and his entries often spoke of his great love and admiration for his "strong, brave, and intelligent wife."

Spread throughout the diary, Benjamin wrote about "the nuisance" as the man was called and his annoying and bothersome behavior. Jackson Best, an old acquaintance of Julia's, followed Julia around town if she happened to be there alone. The man glared menacingly at Benjamin and Julia whenever he saw them in town together. At other times, Best sent small gifts to Julia or offered her a ride to her home in his carriage from her afternoon of shopping in Nantucket town. Julia always refused his offers.

When Lin read the last section of Benjamin's writings, she had to clear her throat several times.

"Jackson Best knocked on my door today with tears streaming down his face. He shouted at me and told me that I was the cause of Julia's death. Best said that Julia always loved him and that she wanted to leave me, but because of her kindness, she was reluctant to do so for fear of breaking my heart. Jackson Best told me that Julia had arranged to meet him on the boat so that they could travel to the mainland and then go on to New York City. Once there, Julia was planning to speak to a lawyer about divorcing me. Best said it was my fault that Julia fell from the boat and drowned. I cannot believe that my sweet wife did not love me, but Best has put a seed of doubt in my mind that I cannot shake. I wander through my duties with my thoughts only on Julia. I feel that my life is over and that I will die from the heavy weight of my grief and sadness. I will not write again in this book. I will bury it behind the wall in the room where Julia and I spent so many happy evenings together."

Viv brushed a tear from her eye. "The man can't cross over to the other side because of his misery. His spirit can't rest. He's stuck in that lighthouse."

Lin said, "I think the ghosts never appear together because Benjamin is afraid that Julia loved Jackson Best."

"I understand what keeps Benjamin here, but why doesn't Julia cross over?" Jeff asked.

All faces turned to Lin.

Lin lifted her hands in a helpless gesture. "Maybe her rage at Best for causing her death is keeping her here?"

"Maybe she is aware that her husband is still wandering around the lighthouse," Anton suggested. "Maybe she is unable to reach him. Perhaps she won't leave without him."

Lin smiled at the historian. "I always knew you were a genius."

Anton blushed.

***

The last light of dusk was fading into darkness while Lin worked on the last design sketch for the wildflower gardens around the keeper's cottage. She kept glancing up at the lighthouse looking for Benjamin Day. Nicky let out a low growl and Lin whirled around to see Jason Grande hurrying towards her.

"Are you here alone?"

Lin was glad her dog was with her. "The others left in the late afternoon for another job. Everyone's gone."

"Why are *you* here?" Grande demanded.

"I stopped by after my last client. I'm finishing a sketch before I head home."

"Help me carry some boxes to the lighthouse." Grande started away. "Unless you're too weak."

Lin bristled at his tone. "I think I'm strong enough to carry some boxes for you ."

Grande was about to retort, but changed his mind. "I need to get these boxes in place before I head to a meeting."

Lin stood beside Grande's van watching him remove several boxes from the hatch and place them on the ground. She refused to move anything until she was asked.

Nicky kept his eyes on the man and several times he let out a low growl.

Grande handed Lin a container and eyed the small creature. "What's wrong with that dog?"

"I don't think he likes you," Lin told him.

Grande scowled. "Well, I don't like animals so the feeling is mutual." When the man reached for the last box, Lin noticed that he seemed to push something under the seat before quickly hitting the button on the van door so it would slide shut. He didn't turn towards Lin until the latch clicked into place.

An icy sensation of dread ran down Lin's throat into her stomach. Grande placed the smaller box on top of the carton that Lin was holding, picked up the other containers from the ground, and led the way down the path.

As Lin watched Grande, something about his movements and body language caused something to ping in her brain, but she couldn't figure out what it was trying to tell her. "What's in these boxes?"

"Things," Grande answered.

When they reached the door to the lighthouse, Grande put his cartons on the ground and then took the ones from Lin's arms. When his hand brushed her skin, a sickening sensation slipped through her veins.

"That's all I needed," Grande said dismissively.

Lin turned to go. "You're welcome."

Nicky let out a bark just as a blast of swirling icy air surrounded Lin.

When she flicked her eyes back to Grande, she almost jumped. The translucent form of Benjamin Day stood a few steps to Grande's right staring at the man and the boxes.

Benjamin looked at Lin, turned his gaze back to Grande and the boxes, and then moved his eyes to

Lin. With a serious expression, he shook his head. When the ghost looked back at Grande, rage burned in his eyes and his atoms turned bright red. With a whoosh, the ghost's glistening particles flared and the heat from his burning atoms washed over Lin.

The ghost was gone.

"What are you staring at?" Grande growled. "I don't need anything more from you."

Lin blinked at the man, disoriented for a moment, then she turned on her heel and jogged down the hill to the keeper's cottage. Nicky gave Grande one last growl before taking off after his owner.

Lin picked up her notebook from the spot where she'd left it when Grande had asked for her help. In the settling darkness, her mind raced a mile a minute as she hurried to the parking lot and to her truck. Approaching the architect's van, Lin glanced towards the lighthouse to see where Grande was and not spotting him in the shadows, she walked close to his vehicle, stopped, turned on the flashlight on her phone, and pressed her face close to the window. Shining the light onto the floor of the van, Lin noticed what looked like gray strands of hair sticking out from under the seat.

Lin took a step back. *Is that a wig? Or something else?*

***

189

J.A Whiting

When Lin walked into Viv's bookstore, she and the dog headed to the office off the hall.

Viv looked up. "Where have you been? I've been texting you for two hours."

Pulling out her phone and seeing her missed messages, Lin groaned. "I forgot to turn the ringer on."

"Sit down." Viv gestured to the chair at the side of the desk and tapped on the keyboard of her laptop. "Wheel that chair over here. I have something to show you."

Peering at the screen, Lin waited anxiously.

"I was looking up Jason Grande to see if I could find anything about his background and why he hated islands." Viv pointed at the screen. "Look at this."

Lin read and her jaw dropped.

Viv nodded. "Jason Grande changed his last name. He used to be Jason Best."

Lin stared at the laptop.

"Guess when he changed it? During the gap year he took off after graduating from college."

"His last name was Best?" Lin looked at Viv. "Is he related to Jackson Best?"

"I'd put money on it. But what does it mean? What's going on?"

Lin nervously pushed her hair back from her face trying to make sense of the news. Images and thoughts pinged in her brain. The strands of a gray wig in the back of Grande's van. The way Grande walked. The man outside her house late at night. The cobra head.

All the bits and fragments of information swirled in her head so quickly that the small office began to spin in her vision and then, one by one, the pieces fell and aligned and nearly completed the puzzle.

The color drained from Lin's face. "Oh, no."

CHAPTER 24

On the ride to the lighthouse, Lin gave Viv a summary of what she was thinking. "I don't know all the "hows" and "whys" but I bet Jason Grande is a relative of Jackson Best. If Jason knows that his uncle, or however Best is related to him, was obsessed with Julia Day, then I bet Jason became obsessed with Best's plight. Best died at the base of the cliff from falling or jumping from the rocks. Jason equates the lighthouse with Best's misery. He must want revenge so he will ruin the lighthouse or hurt anyone who works to restore the light. Benjamin appeared right next to Jason when he corralled me into helping him with those boxes. Benjamin was trying to tell me something."

Viv had one hand clutching Nicky in her lap and her other hand on the dashboard to steady herself from Lin's wild driving. "As I've said a million times before, these ghosts need to learn to talk. Wouldn't it be so much easier for them to just lay it all out there so you knew what was going on?"

"It would be easier, but that's not how it works." Lin yanked on the steering wheel to take the turn and the truck bumped over the windy entranceway.

Darkness had fallen over the landscape by the time Lin and Viv careened into the parking lot of the East End lighthouse and jumped from the vehicle. Theirs was the only car in the lot. No one else was around. With his nose to the ground, Nicky darted back and forth about the space.

"What's the plan?" Viv edged closer to her cousin.

"Let's walk around and make sure things look okay."

Viv groaned. "I knew that would be the answer. Can't we just survey the scene from here?"

Lin sent off a text to Jeff telling him that she and Viv were at the lighthouse because she had the idea that Jason Grande was up to something. Stuffing the phone into her back pocket and flicking on her flashlight, Lin tugged on her cousin's arm and the two started down the hill to the lighthouse. As they walked, an odd sensation bounced against Lin's skin like tiny jolts of static electricity.

The young women stopped in their tracks when they heard Nicky's barking coming from near the keeper's house.

Lin's heart thudded. "Nicky's near the cottage. Let's go there first."

"Wait," Viv's shook. "Look up there. Is that....?"

Lin followed Viv's hand pointing to the top of the lighthouse and she squinted trying to understand what she was be seeing. The clouds had parted momentarily and against the inky night sky, Lin thought she saw a curl of smoke escaping from the top of the lighthouse. "Is it smoke?" Her heart beating like a drum, Lin pulled her phone out and made a "911" call reporting possible smoke coming from East End Light.

Just as she shoved her phone back into her pocket, a blast so loud and strong shook the ground beneath the cousins' feet and tossed them a foot into the air. The girls crashed to the earth.

Pushing herself up, Lin gasped and coughed and crawled on her hands and knees to Viv.

"I'm okay." Viv managed to get the words out. Shaking her head and rubbing her shoulder, she said, "What was that?"

Struggling to her feet, Lin stood agape. Fire licked at the barn's roof. The crackling of burning wood filled the air.

"Where's Nicky?" Lin stumbled down the hill to the keeper's house calling desperately for the little dog.

The roar of the barn fire made it impossible for her to hear if Nicky was barking so when she got to the cottage, she moved from window to window shining the light in through the glass.

"Viv!" Lin shouted as she ran to the front door.

"Kurt's inside. We have to get him out." Lin pulled so hard on the locked door that she lost her balance and tumbled backward.

Viv helped her cousin to her feet. "Let's break a window. We can't budge the door. Look for something to bash it in with."

Lin knew the same thought was in Viv's mind. If the lighthouse was on fire and an explosion just set the barn to flames, what was going to happen to the keeper's house? How much time did they have?

The girls ran around the cottage trying to find a tool or a branch or something to break the window with, and coming up empty, Lin pulled her sweater off, wrapped it around her arm, and held tight to the heavy flashlight. Her panic and fear increased her strength and the window shattered at the first blow. Lin used the flashlight to break the shards out of the casing and then Viv boosted her up to the window so she could crawl through. Lin dropped to the floor with a thud.

"Kurt." She knelt beside the man.

Kurt opened his eyes. Blood trickled from his head. His hands and legs were bound by leather straps. "Lin?" A tiny smile played over his lips. "We have to stop meeting like this."

"We need to get you out of here. The barn just went up in flames." Lin ran to the front door and unlocked it so Viv and Nicky could enter, then she ran to the back room of the building where she knew Jeff had left some of his tools. Grabbing a small saw and a heavy wrench, Lin was about to dart back to the front room when she saw something on the floor that made her blood run cold. A bomb?

Lin raced back to Kurt and Viv and shoved the wrench into Viv's hand. "If anyone comes in here, crack him over the head." Kneeling on the floor, she moved the saw back and forth over Kurt's bonds. "Come on," she shouted at the saw.

Kurt suggested Lin angle the tool to the side and finally the leather strips gave way.

"I think there's a bomb in the back room." Lin's breathing was so labored she could barely speak.

"A bomb?" Viv shrieked. She eyed the front door longingly, but kept herself from sprinting out of the house.

Kurt grabbed the saw and hacked at the binds on his legs. When he broke free, the three people and the dog bolted from the house with Lin and Viv grasping Kurt's arms to assist his escape.

Once at the parking lot, they sank to the ground to catch their breath. Rubbing her face, a cold funnel of air surrounded her and she looked up to see Benjamin standing on the grass near the cliffs. He raised his hand and pointed.

Jason Grande stood perched on the rocks staring out to sea.

Lin pushed to her feet and moved slowly over to

him. "Jason."

Grande whirled and almost lost his balance. "You." His eyes looked wild against his pale face. "You ruined it, didn't you?"

Lin took a step closer. "Why don't you come off the rocks?"

"Don't come over here," Jason raged. "Only the barn. I was only able to destroy the barn. I failed." Tears of anger poured down the man's cheeks. "You stopped the destruction, didn't you?"

The scream of a fire truck or a police car sounded off in the distance.

"I didn't do anything, Jason. Come away from the rocks."

"My great-great-grandfather died down there. Jackson Best. Did you know that? He slipped from these rocks." Grande waved crazily towards the edge of the cliff. "Jackson was in love, but the woman wouldn't see that her life would have been better with him. She resisted his proposals, she married someone else. She ruined his life." Grande pulled at his hair and let out a wail like a wild animal. "I swore I would get revenge on this place. I swore it."

Lin moved closer. "Julia Day didn't love Jackson Best. She loved Benjamin. Jackson was obsessed with something he couldn't have so he pushed Julia off a boat into Nantucket Sound. He pushed her to her death. He murdered her."

Grande stared at Lin for several long moments. "You lie," he sneered. "Just like every woman on this earth."

A fire truck roared into the lot and Lin turned momentarily to look at it. Catching movement from the corner of her eye, she flashed her gaze back to Grande to see him turn in slow motion and leap from the cliff.

"No!" Instinctively, she reached out her hand to him, but he was gone.

Feeling the cold air encircle her, Lin looked to her left. Benjamin stood just a few yards away, staring over the edge of the bluff, his form translucent and shining in the lighthouse's beam.

Tears streamed down the ghost's cheeks.

Making eye contact with Lin, Benjamin put his hand over his heart, gave a slight nod, and disappeared.

CHAPTER 25

Jeff drove his truck through the darkness along Milestone Road on the way to East End Lighthouse with Lin sitting on the passenger side and Nicky resting on the cab's second row seat. They'd just left Anton's house where they'd gathered with Libby and Viv for dinner and to discuss the recent happenings.

Lin invited Viv to come with them to the late-night visit to the lighthouse, but she declined because she was meeting John at his boat as soon as he finished some paperwork at his office. "Anyway," Viv told them with a smile, "I can't see ghosts. You can give me a full report tomorrow." As she was leaving Anton's, Viv hugged Lin and said goodnight. "I hope they're there. I hope this part of the story has a happy ending."

Jason Grande died at the base of the rocks from his jump from the top of the cliffs … just like his great-great-grandfather, Jackson Best, over a hundred and fifty years ago.

"Mr. Grande was as successful as his relative was," Anton said at dinner. "How unfortunate that both men suffered mental illness."

In fact, the issue appeared to run in the family on the male side to varying degrees. Grande had been treated off and on since he was in his late teens for obsessive behavior, paranoia, and depression. Somehow the brilliant architect had become haunted by his great-great-grandfather's misfortunes and he'd made it his mission to avenge the man by destroying the lighthouse, the place that Grande linked to his relative's demise.

Gathered around Anton's dining table, the small group discussed the ghosts.

Libby said, "Benjamin Day's heart was torn apart by the loss of his wife."

"And," Viv added, with a touch of anger in her voice, "by the nagging fear that Julia may not have loved him and really wanted to be with Jackson Best." She shook her head. "Why would Best tell Benjamin such a thing?"

Libby put down her fork. "Best counted Benjamin among the reasons that Julia rejected him so he had to make Benjamin as miserable as he was."

"Benjamin. The poor man." Anton sipped from his wine glass. "He died from a broken heart. His health declined after the loss of his wife. I believe the man was unable to muster the will to live."

"Why would Best take on the job of lighthouse keeper after Benjamin died?" Lines of confusion showed on Jeff's forehead.

Lin had been listening to the ideas and conjecture. "My guess is that Best wanted to live in the house where Julia had spent so much time. His family had already left him. He was alone."

Anton had discovered that Best's obsession with Julia had impacted his many businesses. He'd lost nearly all of his holdings by the time Benjamin died. "In addition, perhaps due to the loss of his fortune, the man needed a place to live and when he approached his friend for the appointment as lighthouse keeper, the friend obliged."

"What about the drawings he made of the woman ghost?" Libby brought up the artwork Best had done in his last year of life. "It must have been Julia appearing to him."

"I don't think she could cross over due to being murdered. I've read that some spirits become stuck after experiencing a violent death." Lin rubbed her forehead. "I recall that Best never drew the ghost-woman at the lighthouse. The scenes showed the spirit in fields, in town, on the roads, near the shoreline, but never at the lighthouse."

"If Benjamin was stuck at the lighthouse, why wouldn't Julia have gone to him there?" Viv questioned.

"It may be," Libby suggested, "that the two

spirits had been torn so violently from one another that their grief and misery prevented them from connecting. Perhaps Julia couldn't bear to return to the place where her husband had died. No one knows the answers to these questions. It's merely speculation."

Viv scowled. "What *isn't* speculation is that Grande was the one who owned that cane with the cobra head." The cane, minus the cobra head, had been found in Jason Grande's van along with a gray wig, a pair of glasses, and some clothes. Grande used the items as a disguise so that he could move about the town without being noticed.

Lin nodded. "He was the one who was at the historical museum looking for information on his relative and Benjamin Day."

"I bet he was the one Kurt saw with a camera near the cliffs at the lighthouse the night I got hit on the head," Jeff said. "Grande must have seen us arrive and then spied on us. I must have been about to run into him near the keeper's cottage so he hit me with his cane and the cobra head came off."

Viv sat straight. "Grande must have been at the lighthouse and saw Lin and Leonard find the cobra head in the grass. He was the one who was outside Lin's house the night she heard noise at the window. He was going to break in to find the cobra head."

A shudder ran down Lin's back as she thought about what might have happened if she'd been asleep when Grande made his attempt to break in. "You know, when I was helping him carry those containers to the lighthouse, I was walking behind him. Something about his movements pinged in my head. I think it was because I recalled following him to his car the night he ran from my house. The way he walked seemed familiar to me. I also spotted the gray hairs of the wig in his van that day." Lin blanched. "Those containers I carried were filled with the explosives Grande used on the buildings and the lighthouse."

Jeff said, "I heard from Kurt that the fire inspectors said that the reason the explosives didn't go off at the keeper's house and the ones in the lighthouse fizzled out couldn't be determined. They called it a stroke of luck."

Smiles formed on the faces of everyone at the table. They all knew the real reason the cottage and lighthouse were spared.

It was Benjamin. He stopped the explosives from igniting. Benjamin saved the structures from destruction.

"What about the barn?" Lin asked. "Can it be saved?"

"Kurt isn't sure yet. It's pretty damaged. Kurt hopes the damaged parts of the building can be reconstructed and the remaining section can be restored."

"Well," Anton raised his glass. "Lin has solved another mystery."

Lin frowned. "I think it solved itself. I did have the sensation that the lighthouse was in danger and I felt that Grande was behind it, but I hadn't yet put all the pieces together."

"I have no doubt you would have." Anton smiled.

Lin returned the historian's smile with a shrug. "I'm not sure about that. Why don't we just drink to a mystery solved?"

The group raised glasses and clinked with each other. There was still one part of the mystery that Lin needed to find out about.

Taking the last turn, Jeff said, "I'm sure glad we never confronted Kurt with our suspicions that he was behind the sabotage at the lighthouse."

Lin let out a sigh of relief. "I'm so happy that Kurt is the man we thought he was."

Kurt told Jeff that he'd suspected Jason Grande all along of trying to sabotage the lighthouse project. He wasn't able to put his finger on anything definitive, but there were a number of reasons to suspect him. Kurt stayed at the project late one night and discovered Grande skulking around the place. Kurt confronted him, Grande acted nervous and got angry. Kurt had noticed Grande coming out of the barn the morning that one of the workers had the accident and fell from the collapsing metal staging. "Grande was carrying a wrench. I wondered why he'd be holding a tool. He was the architect, not a worker. It seemed off."

The night Jeff got hit in the head and they found Kurt hurt in the barn, Kurt's wife had dropped him off at the lighthouse so he could do some detective work. He hoped to catch Grande in action. Kurt had returned to the lighthouse at night many times trying to catch Grande. Until he'd found evidence or proof, Kurt was unwilling to accuse someone so he kept his suspicions to himself.

Jeff pulled his truck to a stop in the dark gravel parking lot. When they got out of the truck, the dog trotted ahead of them as they walked closer to the lighthouse.

"Do you feel cold?" Jeff asked. "Do you sense them?"

"No." Lin's heart dropped. Where was Benjamin? Had Julia found him? Were they together?

They walked around the base of the light, headed to the keeper's cottage, and then over to the barn. Jeff pointed his flashlight at the ruined structure. The smell of burned wood floated on the air.

When she saw how badly damaged the barn was, Lin's hand flew to her chest and a few tears gathered in her eyes. "Is it possible to repair all of this?"

Jeff put his arm around her shoulders.

"Designers, construction workers, electricians, and, oh yes, *carpenters* have the ability to work magic, you know."

Lin smiled. "Yes. I've recently discovered that ... about carpenters, at least."

Nicky stood at the top of the hill and whined.

"He must want to head home." Under the starry sky, Jeff and Lin headed to the parking lot and Lin turned around and took another look at the lighthouse watching it flash its beam into the distance. Staring at the red and white structure standing proud and tall with its light stretching over the sea, Lin felt gratitude that the lighthouse had survived the attempt to destroy it, but her heart was heavy not knowing what had happened to her ghosts.

"I was sure that Benjamin heard me when I spoke to Grande. I was sure he heard me say that Jackson Best had murdered Julia. I was positive he heard me when I said that Julia only loved him." She sighed and they turned away.

Just as Lin had taken a step, air colder than she'd ever felt before engulfed her. "Wait," she whispered.

Nicky let out a happy bark and wagged his tiny tail.

Lin and Jeff faced the lighthouse. She reached for Jeff's hand. "I think they're coming. Hold my hand. Maybe you'll feel them."

The door at the base of the lighthouse opened and the light that flooded out nearly blinded Lin. Two shimmering figures emerged hand in hand.

Nicky barked again and sat at attention watching, his tail swishing back and forth over the gravel.

Not taking her eyes from the two ghosts before her, Lin tightened her grip on Jeff's hand.

"They're here?" he whispered.

Lin squeezed his hand in reply.

In the center of the blazing light, Benjamin and Julia smiled at Lin and then the atoms of their bodies began to shine and glimmer like tiny diamonds dancing on the night air. Slowly the particles began to swirl and sparkle with the most beautiful light Lin had ever seen. The two ghosts' atoms blended together in their ballet, light and delicate, but with a powerful glistening brightness.

Lin stood transfixed. Her body felt as light as a feather, as if it could easily lift off the ground and float over the world.

As the atoms sparkled with every color of the rainbow, they swirled like a tornado and then shot high into the air where they sizzled away like fireworks in a Fourth of July sky.

"They're gone, aren't they?" Jeff asked.

Lin gave the slightest of nods. Electricity seemed to be pulsing through her body filling her with feelings of joy. She pointed to where the ghosts had flashed away.

After a minute of looking up at the sky where the spirits had disappeared, Jeff asked, "Where do they go when they leave the earth?"

"I have no idea." Lin turned to face her boyfriend. "But I know it's good ... and beautiful." She wrapped her arms around her handsome carpenter and he pulled her close, tracing his thumb gently over Lin's cheek.

"Good and beautiful," Jeff said softly ... then he leaned down and lovingly kissed her lips.

THANK YOU FOR READING!

BOOKS BY J.A. WHITING CAN BE
FOUND HERE:

www.amazon.com/author/jawhiting

To hear about new books and book
sales, please sign up for my mailing list
at:

www.jawhitingbooks.com

Your email will never be sold, shared, or
spammed.

BOOKS BY J. A. WHITING

LIN COFFIN COZY MYSTERY SERIES

CLAIRE ROLLINS COZY MYSTERY SERIES

SWEET COVE COZY MYSTERY SERIES

OLIVIA MILLER MYSTERY-THRILLER SERIES (not cozy)

If you enjoyed the book, please consider leaving a review.

A few words are all that's needed.

It would be very much appreciated.

J.A Whiting

ABOUT THE AUTHOR

J.A. Whiting lives with her family in New England.
Whiting loves reading and writing mystery stories.

VISIT ME AT:

www.jawhitingbooks.com

www.facebook.com/jawhitingauthor

www.amazon.com/author/jawhiting

Made in the USA
Middletown, DE
04 February 2017